the
dating
deal
a novel

the dating deal

a novel

by melanie marks

spring creek
BOOK COMPANY
Provo, Utah

© 2005 Melanie Marks

ISBN 13: 978-1-932898-40-8
ISBN 10: 1-932898-40-9
e. 1

Published by:
Spring Creek Book Company
P.O. Box 50355
Provo, Utah 84605-0355

www.springcreekbooks.com

Cover design © Spring Creek Book Company
Cover design by Nicole Cunningham
Cover photo © Sweet Expressions Photography & Michele L. Tolley
Cover model: Aja Marie Gonzalez

Printed in the United States of America
10 9 8 7 6 5 4 3 2 1
Printed on acid-free paper

Library of Congress Cataloging-in-Publication Data

Marks, Melanie, 1967-
The dating deal / by Melanie Marks.
    p. cm.
Summary: When the popular Trent suddenly starts to show interest in her, Megan--a devout Mormon and a gifted singer--is alternately thrilled and confused about his attentions.
ISBN-13: 978-1-932898-40-8 (pbk. : alk. paper)
ISBN-10: 1-932898-40-9 (pbk. : alk. paper)
 [1. Conduct of life--Fiction. 2. Mormons--Fiction. 3. Singers--Fiction. 4. High schools--Fiction. 5. Schools--Fiction. 6. Christian life--Fiction.] I. Title.
PZ7.M3437Dat 2005
[Fic]--dc22
                        2005008800

dedication

To Chris, Taylor, Josh, and Nicole

acknowledgments

A huge, gigantic "thank you" to Tammy Daybell for believing in my book, and another to my wonderful family for being supportive while I wrote it. Thank you!

chapter 1

"And that concludes my report," I said with relief.

All I had left of my oral presentation was one little technicality, one I was tempted to skip. Only I couldn't.

I looked out at the sea of my third-period classmates—or pretended to, anyway. Really, my eyes just swept across the wall at the back of the room, avoiding making any sort of eye contact or actually seeing anyone. (That imagining your audience is only wearing underwear just never worked for me.)

"Uh . . . any questions?"

Aspen Bower quickly raised her hand. "I have one, Megan."

I groaned inwardly. Of course Aspen would have a question for me. She probably sat through my whole presentation searching her ditzy highlighted-blond brain until she came up with something I couldn't possibly answer. That was so Aspen. She was Laura Nolen's best friend. And Laura Nolen was now dating my ex-boyfriend, The Back-Stabbing Snake (or better known to the rest of Jefferson High as Conner, but whatever).

Both Aspen and Laura seemed to have it in for me. But truthfully, come on, shouldn't it have been the other way around?! He dumped *me* for her.

I gritted my teeth. "Yes, Aspen?"

"Now that Conner dumped you, who are you going to the spring dance with?"

I could feel my face turn bright red, not that it wasn't pretty much that shade already. I hated standing at the front of the class. Having everyone stare at me. Giving me their semi-undivided attention—

1

though now, thanks to Aspen, I had everyone's full attention. Trust me, my audience was suddenly captivated. It was like a nightmare come true.

I wished I could shock the catty smirk off Aspen's smug face. I wished I could announce to her and the whole class that I was going to the dance with a hot guy, someone way cooler than Conner. But the brutal truth was, I wasn't going to the dance. With anyone. I was far from over Conner. I was still licking my wounds from our break-up.

But having to admit that to Aspen, I would have rather spontaneously combusted. Only, what could I do? Make up a guy? Actually, I considered doing that. Knowing it was lame wasn't what stopped me. What stopped me was knowing I'd probably get caught in the lie and look even more pathetic.

So instead I stammered, "I'm, uh . . ."

But then a miracle happened. A voice came from out of nowhere, like an angel, sort of.

"She's going with me," the voice announced. It was like an answer to my silent prayer.

I didn't care who the guy was—a dork, a nerd, a frog. I didn't care. I was so grateful for whoever said it I would have gone with him no matter what, just because he saved me.

So I blurted out, "Yeah, I'm going with . . ."

I looked across the room to see who had mercifully come to my rescue. But I froze when I saw who it was, because it wasn't a sweet, heroic dork. It was Trent Ryan. Trent Ryan! Suddenly, I didn't feel relief anymore. Suddenly, I felt panic. Trent was considered "cool" at Jefferson High, and cool people from Jefferson scared me. Even worse, to me, Trent wasn't only "cool" he was "super cool."

Trent was in a cool band. And he had cool hair. And he was adorable, and handsome. All of that kind of stuff. And he dated popular girls: beauty queens and cheerleaders. Not shy girls like me. Girls who blushed if he looked in their general direction. So, what was he doing? Why was he saving me? I was afraid he didn't mean it. Afraid he was only making a joke to compound my turmoil, only he didn't look as though he was making a joke. He looked completely sincere.

Staring into Trent's warm brown eyes, I had to take a leap of faith. Trust him. His earnest gaze seemed to be telling me to do that. And, anyway, what else could I do? Say, "No, I'm not going with Trent"? Admit that my date for next Friday night was a bowl of Chunky Monkey ice cream? Admit that my big plans were to bawl my eyes out?

Locked in Trent's gaze, I prayed I could trust him. Prayed that he wasn't only cool, but nice.

I swallowed. "I'm going with Trent."

That immediately knocked the air out of Aspen's sails.

She whipped around to Trent accusingly. "Since when do you go to school dances?" she asked. And then I remembered—for the briefest of moments, sophomore year, Aspen and Trent had been a couple. They broke up when he refused to take her to a school dance.

"Since I met the right girl," he answered.

I blinked. Huh?

The rest of the class seemed just as shocked. They made shocked noises like, "Oohh" and "Ahh" and . . . shocked noises.

Aspen only narrowed her eyes, glaring at Trent, seeming to say, "I hate you." But she didn't say anything else aloud. Instead she turned back in her seat, staring straight ahead. Boy, she looked mad.

Oh no, what was I in the middle of? Drama scenes weren't really my thing. I just wanted to get through my presentation and back to my seat. That was it.

"Can I—uh, sit down now?" I asked our teacher.

"Sure. Good job, Megan," Ms. Wright said. As I scurried to my seat, she added, "Have fun at the dance."

The words hit me like a thunderbolt. I was going to the dance!!!

I glanced over at my best friend, Nina. She gave me her way-to-go-girl smile, and I knew what she was thinking: eighth grade. Back then Nina and I both had huge, fanatical crushes on Trent. He was new at the time and we read an article interviewing him in our school paper. It said that he liked peanut butter cookies. So Nina and I started making them for him—batches and batches of them—anonymously. We would leave them on his doorstep and run away. And sometimes we would fill his locker with them—literally *fill* it. We were kind of weird back then. But it was fun, and he never found out it was us.

Of course, that was back in eighth grade. I had pretty much gotten over my crush on Trent by now. Pretty much. Except whenever I would hear him sing in his band. Then it was like eighth grade all over again. I would get the urge to make batches of peanut butter cookies, but I learned to resist. After all, I'd never even spoken to the guy, except once. And that was way back at the beginning of the school year. It had been a nice conversation, sweet really, but not exactly something to write a romance novel about. And it was only that once. So, I kept my peanut butter cookie urges in check and went on with my life, hardly ever thinking about Trent.

Until now.

Now I couldn't take my mind off him. I sat in government class totally oblivious to Zack Fry's oral presentation. I couldn't tell you for the life of me what his report was on, or if he was even speaking English. My brain was in a total "Trent fog." All I could think about was Trent. Trent, Trent, Trent. My knight in shining armor.

Was I actually going to the dance with him? Was that for real? Or did he simply see a damsel in distress and decide to come to her rescue?

chapter 2

I sat through the rest of class convincing myself Trent wasn't really taking me to the spring dance. He had simply helped me out of an embarrassing moment and I was nothing but grateful to him, but we *weren't* going to the dance. We weren't. There was no possible way. Trent wasn't that kind of guy, a going-to-the-school-dance kind. He had a creed, a motto. Everyone knew it. It went like this: "I don't do school dances." It was like a rule with him, a rule that demolished astronomical gobs of his short, fleeting romances.

So, I sat through class trying to smack myself with reality, trying to get a grip. Trent didn't go to school dances. He just didn't. And if he ever did, it wouldn't be with me. I wasn't being humble or pessimistic or anything like that. I was being reasonable. As I've already pointed out, we had never actually spoken before—except for that one time at the beginning of the school year. That conversation had clued me into the fact that he was a nice guy, but he hadn't exactly seemed especially interested in me, though maybe he had seemed a *little* interested. Only I hadn't been sure if that was for real or simply wishful thinking. And probably the wishful thinking was it, since he never found the need to talk to me again.

Sitting in class, oblivious to my classmates' presentations, I thought back to that day at the beginning of the school year, the day Trent had waited for me after third period.

"Hey, Megan," he had said as I was coming out of Government.

I looked around, thinking he must be talking to a different Megan—Megan Rollings or someone. Only Megan Rollings wasn't around. Neither was any other Megan. Only me. Still, it took him grasping my arm before I acknowledged him because I had no idea he even knew my name.

"This is for you," Trent said handing me a gift wrapped in purple paper. I stared at it a moment, amazed. Speechless. Trent Ryan was giving me a gift?

He grinned at my puzzled expression. "It's not from me. It's from my sister, Wendy."

I widened my eyes. "Wendy's your sister?"

Over the summer, I had worked at a day camp for children with Down Syndrome. Wendy had been my very favorite camper. She was so sweet and fun. She had talked my ear off about her older brother, Charlie. But I didn't recall her mentioning Trent. Not once. Believe me, I'd remember if she had.

"Yeah." Trent smiled, as though he was really fond of Wendy. That brought my residual crush feelings for him gurgling up to the surface. "Wendy, she's my buddy."

"And you have a brother? Charlie?"

"Oh." Trent looked around the crowded hallway, and then said, sort of confidential-like, "I'm Charlie."

I looked at him with confusion.

He smiled again. "Charles is my first name. Trent, my second, but obviously, I go by that, except at home. There I'm Charlie."

"Oh."

"You might want to keep that information to yourself," Trent said.

I nodded, smiling. "Okay. But Wendy sure loves you. She talked about you all the time."

"Yeah?" Trent stared into my eyes, making me feel wobbly. "She talked about you a lot, too."

Now this is the part I'm not quite clear on. We stood staring at each other for a moment. To me it was a magical moment full of blooming affection. But I don't know. Maybe it was just an awkward lull in the conversation and my head wasn't screwed on quite right. I'm not sure.

Finally, Trent spoke. "Are you going to open it?"

"Open?" I glanced down to where his eyes had wandered—the wrapped gift in my hands. Duh! "Oh," I said, quickly opening the package.

It was a Winnie the Pooh journal with a purple pen.

"Wendy said you like Winnie the Pooh and purple," Trent explained. "And she said you like to write poems and stuff. So, I guess she thought you could write them in there."

I smiled, touched by the gift. "Tell her thank you so much."

Trent stuck his hands in his front pockets, gazing into my eyes. "I will. Or you could tell her."

"Oh. Yeah."

We stared at each other again. "Well, I don't want to make you late for class," Trent said, backing away. "See ya."

Then he was gone, lost into the crowded hall of students, and I was left with my heart beating wild and out of control.

But that had been months and months ago and Trent hadn't said another word to me since. Not until today when he said I was going to the dance with him—and he hadn't even said that to me, really. He had said it to Aspen and the class.

It had sure been nice of him, though, to come to my rescue like that. I owed him, big time. I thought about making him some peanut butter cookies after school, maybe not even anonymously. Maybe I would give them to him in person. Or maybe not. Maybe I could just write him a nice thank you note to go along with the cookies and leave them on his doorstep.

Trent came up to me after class, once everyone had left. "So, we're going to the dance?"

"Oh, that's okay," I said, gathering up the visual aids from my presentation. "You don't have to take me. I appreciate it, though. I mean, you really helped me out."

"Then help me out," he said softly.

"Huh?"

"Come with me to the dance. Caitlin and I just broke up. I need a date, you need a date. Let's just . . . date."

I smiled, so pleased I felt I could float away. It wasn't just a sweet ruse to get Aspen off my case, after all. He really meant it. We were going to the dance. Together. For real.

"Okay," I whispered.

Trent grabbed my arm, pulling me back as I started to skip away. "Also, I was thinking. Maybe we could take this thing a step further, I mean more than just the dance."

I tilted my head at him questioningly.

"I mean, you want to get Conner back, right? I think you can. You just need to let him see what he's missing, what a great girl you are."

I stared at him with surprise. How did he know I wanted Conner back? And how could he possibly know what a great girl I am? This was only the second time he'd ever spoken to me in my entire life.

"Are you doing this because of Wendy—for Wendy?"

Trent blinked. "No. This isn't a noble gesture or anything. I don't do stuff like that. It's a deal. We're making a deal. You want to get Conner back, and I want to bug Caitlin. Trust me, you and me dating, that would bug Caitlin."

What did *that* mean?! "Why?"

He laughed. "You know, how you're Miss Goodness and Light— it bugs her."

I dropped my jaw. "I'm Miss Goodness and Light?"

"Look, don't take it the wrong way," he said, although I couldn't see any other way to take it. After all, he said I bugged Caitlin. Apparently, I was annoying. "Anyway, do we have a deal?"

"I don't think so," I said.

Trent furrowed his brow, looking discouraged. "Why not?"

"First of all, Conner might fall for the dance thing. Maybe. It would look like both of us desperate for last minute dates. I can see him reasoning how that could happen. But us getting together for real? He wouldn't buy it."

"Why not?"

"Because he knows me. You're not my type."

Trent ran his hands through his hair, looking impatient. "What's your type? I can be your type."

I grinned at his confidence. "No you can't. Look, I'm Mormon. 'Megan the Mormon,' that's what they call me. Haven't you heard?" Maybe he hadn't. Jefferson was a big school and I wasn't exactly the talk of it—though, apparently, I was more so than I'd thought. I had no idea I was "Miss Goodness and Light."

"Yeah. So?"

"So, I don't drink or go to parties, and I don't date guys who drink and go to parties. I only date Mormons. Conner knows that."

Suddenly, I saw a huge flaw with the whole dance idea. Trent wasn't going to enjoy it. Besides the fact he didn't go to school dances, he didn't date girls like me either. After all, I wasn't going to spike the punch or have a make-out session with him. I wasn't a wild party girl. Far from it. I was . . . Megan the Mormon.

"You probably don't even want to go to the dance with me," I told him. "It's not only that you're not my type, I'm not yours either. Like I said, I don't go to your type of parties, and I don't drink."

"Well, maybe you should," Trent said. "It could help you get your mind off Conner. Help you relax."

I rolled my eyes because that was just stupid, but also because why oh why did he know I was still moaning over Conner? How did he know that? I tried my hardest to appear indifferent to Conner. Why didn't I seem to fool anyone?—*anyone*—not even a guy that had no interest in me whatsoever until today when he saw an opportunity to bug his ex-girlfriend?

The conversation was quickly filling my stomach with knots. I didn't want to talk about it anymore. Conner had hurt me, betrayed me. I shouldn't want him back anyway, but faking a relationship with a guy I was attracted to—one that was bad for me—it didn't seem like a good idea. It just didn't.

"Well, see ya around," I said.

I started to walk away, but Trent grabbed my arm. "I was just messing with your head," he said. "I won't drink, okay? I'm not an alcoholic or anything. I can go a night without drinking."

I sighed. "And you'd be willing to do that?"

He nodded. "Sure. I'll do it. So you'll go with me?"

chapter 3

I sat in the cafeteria, slurping tomato soup from my thermos, only half listening as Nina gushed on and on about how romantic it was that Trent was taking me to the spring dance. Blah, blah, blah.

"He's only taking me to annoy his ex-girlfriend," I reminded her for the hundredth time. "It's not exactly romance material."

Nina shrugged. "It kind of is. Megan, he's taking you to the *dance*. Trent doesn't go to school dances."

Couldn't argue with that. So I didn't bother.

But I figured Caitlin must have really broken his heart. Otherwise, why was he taking such extreme measures to make her jealous or whatever he was doing? Still, no matter the story, I couldn't work up much excitement about the date. The whole thing had me sweating. First of all, would Trent keep his word about not drinking? I didn't want to have to get into an argument about that. It would be just so much easier to avoid the situation, to not go to the dance. And there was "second of all" looming over my head too. I was too infatuated with Trent to be the first girl he ever took to a school dance. Everyone would be watching and I would be a spaz.

I sighed.

Nina nudged me, trying to cheer me up. "It was sweet of him to come to your rescue in class." She grinned. "He slammed Aspen big time."

That lifted my spirits considerably. I grinned, snatching a french fry from Nina's tray. "That he did."

Just then Conner walked by holding hands with Laura. Seeing them together, so couple-ish, was like having a knife jabbed into my

10

heart. Oh the pain! I could have cried right then and there, right in the middle of the cafeteria. Only suddenly, there was a reassuring arm around my shoulders.

"Don't look sad," Trent advised in my ear. Suddenly he was right beside me.

I swallowed, shocked to have Trent Ryan—Trent Ryan!—sitting so close, whispering in my ear, WITH HIS ARM AROUND ME.

"Do I look sad?"

Trent grinned. "Well, now you don't. Now you look shocked. But yeah, you looked sad."

I gazed down at the table. I *was* sad. Conner—or The Back-Stabbing Snake— whatever you want to call him, was my very first boyfriend. The only one I ever had, ever. And he had hurt me, really bad. I didn't know how to act. It wasn't something I could help. It was simply a fact: seeing him with Laura caused me pain.

"He's looking at you," Trent said. "Look at me. Look into my eyes."

I did as Trent advised, but he had no idea at what cost. Staring into his warm brown eyes brought my crush on him zooming back to the surface, as though it had never gone away. My heart was suddenly doing flip-flops.

"I'm going to make you cookies," I told him, warningly.

Trent smiled. "Well, don't panic, but I'm going to kiss you."

Of course, that *did* make me panic. I lurched away from him so fast he kind of fell forward.

"I'm—I'm sure that's not necessary," I stammered, backing away even further. "I'm sure Conner gets the point."

Trent looked amused. "Is it really that scary to you, being kissed by another guy?"

The way his eyes twinkled made me blush. But the thing was, this was all a game to Trent. And even if it wasn't, (which, of course it *was*) he was all wrong for me. I didn't want to get too attached.

"Look, no kissing okay?"

Trent still looked amused. "Relax." He snatched a french fry from Nina's tray, his eyes never leaving mine. "So what kind of cookies are you going to make me?"

I was so flustered I was about to blurt, "Peanut butter," but Nina gave me a quick—necessary—kick under the table.

"What's your favorite?" I asked instead, all wide-eyed and innocent.

chapter 4

After lunch, I drifted out of the cafeteria, feeling wobbly after spending so much time staring into Trent's gorgeous eyes. They were warm and brown, like . . . root beer.

I spotted Brian Abbott just outside the cafeteria door. He was with his girlfriend, Raven. They were deep in conversation. I didn't want to disturb them, but . . .

"Hey, Brian," I said. "Don't forget we're practicing our duet after school."

"Oh yeah, right." Brian smiled. "I won't forget."

I kept moving. I didn't want to make a nuisance of myself. I just wanted him to make it to the practice. I *needed* him to make it.

Brian called after me, "Did you bake more cookies?"

I grinned, turning back to him. "You'll have to come to the practice to find out."

Actually, I had a baggie of chocolate chip cookies in my locker with his name on it. Incentive cookies. I found it was way easier to get him to come to my practices if I baked for them. It worked tons better than my old tactic: begging and pleading.

"Don't worry. I'll be there." Brian's smile broadened. But Raven (I'm sure of it this time) gave me a dirty look. It made me feel funny. What was that about? I didn't know how to ask. Instead, I clumsily backed away.

"Well, see ya."

I staggered to Chemistry class, wounded. It seemed the other day Raven had given me a dirty look as well. But it had happened so quickly and unexpectedly, I hadn't been quite sure. I had pretty much

13

decided it was just my imagination. But this time I was positive, she *scowled* at me. Why?

Today was turning into a total trauma-fest.

It hurt, you know, finding out I was even *more* unpopular than I'd thought. (And believe me, I'd had no delusions of being Miss Popularity.) It hurt learning people found me annoying, that they fully disliked me. Sure, there was Laura and Aspen. I'd known about them. They despised me. No joke. But Raven? What was that about?

And it sure didn't sound as though Caitlin liked me either—and she didn't even know me, at all. What was the *matter* with me?

When I got to Chemistry I didn't have time to think about it anymore because we had to get into groups of three for our lab assignment. For some inexplicable reason, Jasmine Chase chose to be in mine and Nina's group.

"We're pretty lost in this class," Nina warned her.

In all honesty, that wasn't *exactly* true. We could hold our own in the theory part. It was when it came to actually mixing chemicals that things habitually went wrong. Very wrong. Needless to say, neither Nina nor I held out much hope for becoming great scientists. We just crossed our fingers, and prayed for a miracle, to pass the class.

But Jasmine didn't seem to mind. In fact, she seemed to have absolutely no problem with our lack of chem-skill. In fact, unfortunately for her, she fit right into our group, and we bonded. Because when it came to chemistry, we soon learned, the three of us had something in common—confusion.

On our first assignment, Jasmine gave our experiment a tentative whiff as she held our test tube over the Bunsen burner. "Yuck!" She wrinkled her nose. "It stinks."

We were supposed to be making banana oil. But it had turned dark purple, almost black, not at all like the other students' in our class.

"Well, it says here," I stated, quoting the lab manual, "the musk is supposed to be clear and sweet smelling, like a banana."

"Well, it's not clear," Nina observed.

"And it doesn't smell sweet," Jasmine said.

She furrowed her brow. "We did something wrong."

I laughed. "You think?"

Of course then we had to do our usual write up—the infamous "Results of Shame." Admit we screwed up, yet again. Sad, sad, sad. But mostly because it took our new lab sister, Jasmine, by surprise. She was woefully hopeful.

"We could just *write* that it worked out, that it turned clear and sweet smelling like a banana."

Nina and I looked at each other. Poor Jasmine. She didn't get it. Guess we should have warned her: She was working with "Goodness and Light."

"We *could* do that," I admitted, "only, we can't."

Nina and I knew it was routine (even customary) for the class to fudge on experiment results. We saw it done all the time. And I have to admit, sometimes it was sorely tempting, especially because our teacher, Mr. Gregg, often used our results for comic relief. But you know, the musk just didn't turn clear *or* sweet smelling. Or anything remotely close.

So, after comforting poor bewildered Jasmine, we penned our usual messed up results and moved on to our next assignment. It was the Mormon way. (We're sturdy, stalwart people—even in chemistry.) Carry On, Carry On, Carry On!

During the entire period Nina and Jasmine gabbed non-stop about Trent taking me to the dance, which could explain why we botched each and every experiment. Hearing their excitement made it hard for me to keep my feet firmly planted on the ground. It was weird. One moment I was having anxiety attacks, the next I was delirious with excitement. But I tried to keep my excitement in check, at least I gave it my best shot. After all, it was just a "deal," right? And I'd gone over it a hundred times, Trent wasn't someone I could date. No matter how cute or surprisingly nice he was, it didn't change anything. He was still Trent Ryan, Mr. Party Guy. Mr. Heartbreaker. He just wasn't someone that would be good for me, at all. He was the total opposite. But still, I couldn't help it, my heart sped up every time I thought about him. He had come to my rescue twice today: during class, and then again in the cafeteria. And he had been so sweet and his eyes had looked so sincere and, I couldn't help it, I felt delight/excitement/ delirious bliss thinking about him taking me to the dance, taking me into his arms. It had my heart galloping like a racehorse.

"Oh this is bad," I told myself. "This is very, very bad."

*   *   *   *   *

After school, Brian was waiting for me in the choir room, just as he had promised. Seeing him at the piano, I gave a sigh of relief. Sometimes it was hard to get him to come—even with the incentive of cookies. However, I had to admit, lately he was really good about showing. Thank goodness. I guess he was getting into the spirit of things.

See, Brian was my duet partner in honor choir. Lately, I had been forcing practices on him like a madwoman. The thing was, it was important to me that we win this semester's duet competition. Embarrassingly important. Okay, I admit it: I had no life. No social life anyway. All I had these days was music. Music, music, music. And a drive to win this semester's duet competition.

The competition was a regional thing. Last semester Hailey Sheets, from Roosevelt High, won. But that was only because Brian got sick. At the last moment I was stuck pairing up with Phil West. Phil West! Grrrr. He's a nice guy, the best. But the boy can't hold a tune.

Anyway, I couldn't let Hailey win this semester. I couldn't. Not again. I had gone to elementary school with her, and even back then she was so smug about her singing. She got the lead part— Dorothy—in our school's production of *The Wizard of Oz*. I was her understudy but ended up going on as a munchkin. The last night of the play she said I couldn't have "held up" as Dorothy anyway. Whatever that meant.

Then she got to sing the solo at our elementary school graduation, but the way she got it was so extremely cruel and unfair and . . . mean.

She started making fun of me during my audition. She taunted me and giggled with her friends. She made me so self-conscience that I could barely hold back tears, let alone sing.

Then (hurray!) junior high rolled around. I found myself amazingly blessed. Hailey moved and went to a different school. That's when I started to blossom as a singer and in high school I fully bloomed.

Blossomed, bloomed—ha!

I thought, "Hey, I'm over my Hailey insecurities."

But last semester, Hailey made a return, showing up at the regional competition. And drat it all if she didn't win, making her head three thousand times bigger.

After the competition, she told me, "You have a sweet voice, Megan." Then she smiled her wicked, smug smile, "Maybe *too* sweet."

I vowed then and there I would win this semester. And I was going to, even if I had to work Brian twenty-four hours a day to do it.

"Thank you so much for coming," I gushed to Brian now, handing him his bag of cookies. "Don't you think we're getting really good?"

"Yeah. We're great," Brian said, munching on a cookie. "We're going to win for sure."

I bit my lip. It wasn't really "for sure." If it was, I wouldn't be hounding him night and day to practice. We were really good, though. That *was* "for sure."

To be honest, I felt pretty confident we would win. But that wasn't good enough. We had to win. I had to—had to—for once in my life, beat Hailey. I think I probably had something subconscious going on inside me, something to do with losing Conner. It was when we broke up that I turned fanatical about the competition. (And when I say fanatical, I'm not even slightly exaggerating—I was out of control.)

However, I didn't seek therapy about my compulsion (though, Brian probably wished I did), or dwell on my reasons. All I knew was, I had to win. And although Brian and I were sort of terrific, I still worried that something was missing. Every day or so I added new steps to our number, and still racked my brain for extra touches. Mom helped me put together cute matching costumes. Brian's had suspenders and a straw hat. We looked great, sounded great, but still . . .

Hailey and Todd had been partners forever. Last semester, they had a great routine. And they'd had all this semester to practice it, perfect it.

"Let's get busy," I told Brian.

I felt slightly guilty about being so compulsive. I knew Brian used to groan every time he saw me coming his way. He'd whisper something to Raven like, "Oh no, here she comes." And they'd duck around a corner (as if that could stop me).

I knew I was asking too much of him—begging him to practice all the time. After all, he had a girlfriend and a life. Face it, he wasn't obsessed with the competition. He undoubtedly wished he had a partner that wasn't either.

But today Brian surprised me. He didn't act impatient at all to get practice over. In fact, afterwards he stood around talking with me. Actually, he'd started doing that a lot lately. I guess I was growing on him. Or he was getting excited about the competition. Or maybe a little of both. Anyway, I was glad he wasn't moaning about practices anymore.

Only, he was kind of a chatty guy. And I wanted to leave. But I didn't see how to make a smooth getaway. I mean, I'd made him take hours and hours out of his life to come to all of my rehearsals. And I was making him do a dance now for the duet and wear a straw hat. How could I cut his friendly chatter short? I didn't feel I could. It didn't seem fair, or polite.

So, with an inward sigh, I stared into his eyes, trying to appear deeply interested in the lengthy story he was telling me about the time he got lost while camping and tried to catch a fish with his bare hands. I nodded my head, and gasped, "You're kidding!" a lot as though I was fascinated, but through the whole, drawn-out, gabby tale I was speculating, "How can I get out of here?"

Finally, Raven came to my rescue. She looked perturbed at seeing the two us together, giving me another dirty look as she linked her arm through Brian's.

"Are you done with my boyfriend yet?"

"Uh, yeah," I said. And I finally got it, what her dirty looks were about. She thought I was scamming on Brian!

chapter 5

After duet practice, I was kneeling on the kitchen counter, getting out cookie ingredients, when the phone rang. I hopped down, wiping the flour from my hands onto my jeans before answering, "Hello?"

"Hi Megan."

The bottom dropped out of my stomach. It was Conner.

I stood frozen, unable to breathe. He called.

I'd dreamed of this moment. Dreamed of him calling. Dreamed of me acting cool and calm and composed. Only I didn't feel cool or calm or composed. I felt unhinged and unprepared and . . . sweaty.

But that wasn't all. Nothing went the way I dreamed of, or planned. The first words out of Conner's mouth were, "What are you doing hanging out with that guy, Trent Ryan?"

I paced around the kitchen, trying to gather my thoughts. I was too unprepared for his phone call, for the question.

"We're . . . I mean, uh . . ."

Conner didn't wait for coherence. Instead he shot out another question, sounding just as accusatory. "What about your only-dating-Mormons-rule? What happened to that?"

I was about to tell him about "The Deal." I started to get the words out and everything. But then I thought—*Hey!*

The deal was working! One little lunch encounter with Trent had Conner on the phone, dialing my number. He hadn't called once since we'd broken up almost two months ago. But now, suddenly, he was all hot and bothered.

So, even though I hated him thinking less of me, thinking I lowered my standards, I didn't blurt out The Deal. Instead, I did this really brilliant thing that I do in times of crisis: I didn't say *anything*. I just chewed on my lip.

Getting only silence, Conner went on, but he didn't sound accusatory now. He sounded concerned. "Megan, don't get into something you're going to regret. You don't know Trent Ryan, he's . . ."

"What?"

"He's a player. He leads girls on, then hurts them."

I bit my lip, touched that he was concerned for me. It was nice.

When I didn't say anything, Conner went on. "You're in a fragile state right now. It's only been a couple months. You should give yourself time before you jump into anything."

Tears started to form in my eyes. Still, I managed to choke out, "I'm not jumping into anything."

"That's not what I heard," Conner said. "I heard you're going to the dance with him. And the way the two of you were acting in the cafeteria . . ."

Huh?! The way we were acting in the cafeteria? Except for that almost-kiss, we had just sat together, talking.

"Trent's a nice guy," I murmured.

Conner snorted. "Come on Megan, you can't really believe that." Then he sounded more coaxing. "Megan, you've lived a sheltered life. You don't know what normal high school guys are like. You have no idea. But Trent Ryan, geez, Megan the guy's a total player."

Of course I had heard the rumors about Trent roaming from girl to girl, breaking hearts, but today he had seemed nothing but sweet. He had come to my rescue not once, but twice.

Sure, Trent refused to admit it because it didn't go with his "cool" image, but he was a nice guy. He just was. I knew it. My proof wasn't only his rescuing me. There was Wendy to consider, as well. She worshipped Trent. And she'd talked about him all summer long, how sweet he was and all the kind things he did. Obviously, he was a good guy.

But, of course, I understood what Conner was trying to warn me about. I knew when it came to a girl's heart Trent was bad news.

He had a short attention span. Right when every one of his girlfriends thought she was in love, Trent was off in search of another girl. I could have saved Conner the trouble of worrying. All I had to do was explain "The Deal."

But I didn't wanna.

"Conner," I said softly instead, almost ready to cry because what I was going to tell him was the truth. And the truth was kind of brutal. "We're not together anymore. You don't have a say in who I choose to date. And if you think I'm making a mistake, well, you can't expect me to worry about that. I mean, I think *you're* making a mistake dating Laura. And I didn't see you 'give yourself time' before you jumped into anything."

Conner was silent for a moment. Then he sighed with bitter resignation. "Well, don't say I didn't warn you."

chapter 6

I stood staring at the phone long after I'd hung up with Conner. Finally, I wiped away the last of my tears. At least there had only been a few trickles, not a huge downpour. Progress, right? Maybe I was starting to get over him.

Maybe.

I gave a sigh as I went back to making Trent's peanut butter cookies. "If only it were true," I muttered.

If only I was over him. If only I didn't care when I saw him with Laura. If only it didn't break my heart. If only, if only. Grrrr!

Still, I had to admit, "The Deal" was helping—in more ways than one. Besides getting Aspen off my back, and giving my ex-snake-of-a-boyfriend the desperate need to call me for a change, it also gave me something to do besides cry over our break up. Look at me! Here I was just off the phone with Conner, and I wasn't bawling my eyes out. I wasn't. Instead I was baking cookies. And I actually found myself humming as I plopped mounds of dough onto the cookie sheet. Humming! What an amazing, beautiful thing. I hadn't hummed in months. Not since Conner pulled me aside after seminary, saying, "Megan, we need to talk."

I'd just set the timer for the cookies when I heard Mom's car pull into the driveway. Only moments later, my younger brother, Seth, came bounding through the front door, his never-without-it basketball tucked securely under his arm. Mom was in tow, having chauffeured him home from practice.

"I heard you're going to the school dance with Trent Ryan," Seth said, twirling the basketball on his index finger.

I widened my eyes with surprise. So, did Mom.

"Where did you hear that?" I asked at the same moment Mom gushed, "You're going to the dance?"

"Maybe," I murmured, still not quite believing it, and amazed Seth knew anything about it. He was in junior high. His school was twenty minutes away from mine.

"Where did you hear about the dance?" I repeated to Seth.

He shrugged. "At basketball practice. Our assistant coach goes to Jefferson."

Jefferson High is my school. So that cleared things up, sort of. Only, people were talking about me going to the dance with Trent? Everyone knew? Even basketball players? Yikes!

"Why would Trent Ryan take *you?*" Seth asked bluntly, seeming sincerely (not to mention completely) baffled by the concept.

"Why *wouldn't* he take her?" Mom said hurriedly.

She was always doing that these days—jumping in at the first sign of a situation that might, possibly, make me feel even more pathetic than I already did. Being dumped isn't exactly an ego booster.

"Your sister is a bright, beautiful girl," Mom professed. "Any boy would be *lucky* to take her to the dance."

Seth gave Mom a look that said, "Whatever." Then, spinning the ball on his finger again, he said, "But Trent Ryan's *cool.* He's in this awesome, cool band, Baggage. They rock."

"Well, your sister's very musical, too," Mom said, making it sound as though that solved the whole "Why Megan?" mystery. But I could tell Seth's remarks about Trent had her worried. I could tell she was inwardly shaken, inwardly asking, "Is he Mormon?" But all she said to Seth was, "This Trent obviously realizes he and Megan have a lot in common."

My little brother (who's way taller than me)—who I used to push for hours and hours and hours on our backyard swing, and kill *spiders* for—smirked, playfully. "They don't have anything in common, Trent's cool."

"Hey!" I grabbed an oven mitt, throwing it at the towering twerp as he ran upstairs.

Then I turned to Mom. She looked happy for me, happy that I was asked to the dance, but she looked doubtful as well.

"Is this Trent a Mormon?"

I could tell she pretty much already knew the answer.

I shook my head, then quietly, so Seth couldn't hear, explained, "Trent and I made this deal ..."

I told Mom all about class today; about Aspen being a jerk and Trent coming to my rescue, ending the convoluted tale by stressing, "Trent *promised* not to drink."

Mom still looked dubious. "I'll have to talk this over with your dad," she said, visibly conflicted. I knew she didn't want to have to axe my date plans, not when she knew the torture I was under seeing Conner with Laura everyday at school. But . . . Trent wasn't Mormon.

I knew Mom's dilemma. It was my dilemma too.

Still, I went on, pleading my case, and I sounded way more confident about it than I actually felt. "We're not going to start dating or anything," I stressed. "It's just one night. Just a dance."

Right?

*   *   *   *   *

After baking the cookies, I put them into a zip-lock baggie. I thought about dropping them off at Trent's on my way to mutual, but chickened out. I couldn't see myself knocking on his door and actually waiting for him to answer. I knew me, it'd be like eighth grade all over again. I'd take off running.

I really am a coward. I couldn't even go to Wendy's house that day at the beginning of the school year to thank her for the Winnie the Pooh diary. I guess because Trent had gotten my heart beating all wild and crazy when he gave me her gift. It had me feeling guilty, since back then Conner and I had still been together.

That's why I had been too afraid to go to Wendy's house. I was afraid I would run into Trent. And I was afraid I might actually like him, you know, more than just as an eighth-grade crush. So, I had written Wendy a thank you note instead, mailing it to her along with a silly poem I had entitled, "Wendy." I figured she would get a kick out of it. The poem was cute, just like her.

But now my reasons for not going to Trent's had nothing to do with guilt. It was simply fear. I was afraid to show up at his house, afraid he might think I was a dork. Or maybe he would worry I was going to start stalking him. I felt kind of like I was doing that to Conner—stalking him. I would go out of my way any time I left my house to drive by his. I don't even know what I thought I was accomplishing. Seeing if he was home? Seeing if Laura's car was there? I didn't know. The whole thing made me pretty sure I needed psychiatric attention. Still I did it anyway. Even now. Tonight, on my way to mutual.

"So much for being over him," I muttered, remembering what I'd tried telling myself earlier. When I got off the phone with Conner today, having only shed a few tears, I'd thought that maybe it was finally happening—maybe I was finally getting over him. *Still, maybe I am*, I told myself as I drove by his house. Only super slowly.

"At least today I sort of have a reason for driving by," I consoled myself.

I wanted to see if Conner's car was there. Prepare myself in case he actually showed up at mutual, not that I expected him to. His dad was a non-member and Conner had been fairly inactive until he started dating me. Conner's mom, Sister Mathews, loved me—I'd gotten her son active again. But now that we were broken up, Conner had, for the most part, slipped back into inactive status, though occasionally he still showed up for things.

He didn't show up tonight, though. Not that it was a joint activity anyway. It had no impact on me. But it made me sad that Conner was falling away from the church.

For our class activity we practiced a song we were going to be singing in sacrament meeting Sunday. It was called *The Road Home*. I wrote it myself, even the piano accompaniment. We had sung it for achievement night, and afterwards Bishop Woodland asked us to sing it in sacrament meeting.

"Your song was so beautiful, it made me cry," Sister Woodland had said still sniffling. Actually, a lot of people had told me that. Everyone, in fact. I hadn't realized it was going to affect people so strongly. But it was nice because the song meant a lot to me.

After we finished practicing tonight, I was excited. We sounded really good. Three of us were in honor choir together, and the other three had good voices, even if they claimed they didn't. We sounded awesome. I could hardly wait for Sunday.

As I was gathering my stuff to leave, Audrey Tolley wandered over to me, smiling and looking excited. "I heard you're going to the spring dance with Trent Ryan."

I widened my eyes in surprise. "You did?"

I couldn't get over it—how fast word traveled at our school. I mean, Audrey and I didn't run in the same circles (her being popular and everything) and we didn't have any classes together. But, then again, even the junior high was talking about Trent and me. So, I guess I shouldn't have been so surprised.

Audrey nodded with a smile. "Trent's adorable. I'm jealous."

"I . . ."

I was about to tell her not to be. I was about to explain Trent's scam to bug Caitlin. But at the last moment, I decided not to. Audrey was beautiful and popular. I could stand to let her be jealous of me for a change. Besides, I guess "The Deal" was supposed to be a secret. The only person who knew besides Trent and me was Nina.

So, with my "I . . ." still hanging out there, instead of blabbing my secret, I made a quick change of plans, "like your shirt."

chapter 7

Today I planned to give Trent his cookies after third period, but when class was over, I couldn't bring myself to do it. I would have had to say something like, "Hey, Trent, wait up," or something like that. And I couldn't get the words out. Instead, I just watched him walk away, feeling like a dork/coward.

Maybe that's why it was so hard for me to let go of Conner. He was the only boy I felt comfortable around. And that was only because we had been together for so long. It was different when he first moved into our ward. I hadn't really paid that much attention to him. In fact, I couldn't even remember his name. All I could remember was that it started with a "C." I used to call him all sorts of strange things—Corey, Conrad, Chris. Then, once, at a joint activity for mutual, I had to announce his name for a skit. Only I introduced him as Cody. Everyone laughed, including him, but I didn't even realize what I'd done. His name *wasn't* Cody?

Afterwards, I apologized.

"That's okay," he said. "You can call me whatever you want." He looked into my eyes. "Just call me, okay?"

I'd stared up at him with surprise, and he smiled. "Or I could call you," he said. "Only I guess you wouldn't know who I was, the name's *Conner*."

"Conner. Right," I murmured, my mind trying to grasp what was happening. I'd just turned sixteen. Finally old enough to date. The only problem was, I looked about twelve. But, looks aside, I *could* date if I wanted. Only no one seemed interested. Until now. Conner seemed interested.

"I was wondering if you want to go to the game with me tomorrow," he said. "You can call me Cody if you want."

And so that's what I always called him, Cody. I don't think I ever called him Conner once. Not back then, while we were dating. But now things are different. Now I take great effort to think of him as "Conner." After all, we aren't together anymore. Now he's supposed to be just a boy to me, like any other. Nothing special. So I revoked his special name. Only, it's still kind of hard for me to think of him as Conner. In my heart, it seems he'll always be Cody.

*　*　*　*　*

"I can't believe you wimped out on giving Trent his cookies," Nina complained at lunch. "You promised. And it would have been your first time to give him cookies in person. It would have been like a stepping stone or something."

I looked at her like, huh?

"Well, you know, we used to give them to him anonymously. But now, it was going to be like a new phase in your life, giving them to him in person. A milestone, saying, 'You've come a long ways, Baby' or something like that."

I got what she was saying. I did. And, yeah, maybe it would have been a maturity thing for me, a turning of the page in my book of life or whatever. Maybe. But I didn't have time to think about it because just then Trent sat down beside me and my brain turned to Jell-O.

"Where's my cookies?" he said.

"Cody called me yesterday!" I told him excitedly, getting the cookies out of my backpack.

Trent raised an eyebrow at me quizzically, "Who?"

"Oh, um—Conner."

Trent grinned. "No wonder you guys broke up. You can't even remember the poor guy's name."

"That's her 'special' name for him," Nina explained. "She's been calling him that forever."

"But not anymore," I told them, as though I had made a life

altering decision. "He's lost his 'special name' privileges."

"Whoa. Tough love," Trent said with a grin.

I ignored his teasing, too pleased about Conner's call. "Anyway, he called me. He was upset about our act in the cafeteria yesterday."

Trent raised his eyebrows. "Just think if I would have kissed you. He would be yours right now and you wouldn't even be stuck going to the dance with me."

He said that as though going to the dance with him was a major chore I had to endure. But I knew he didn't really believe that. I was pretty sure he knew I had a crush on him. I'm a blusher; it gives stuff like that away.

"These are good cookies." Trent gave them a once over, suddenly seeming amused.

I gave a nervous laugh. "What's so funny?"

"Nothing. I was just remembering something. Back in the eighth grade, I used to get my locker raided with peanut butter cookies." He gave a little laugh. "Not that I'm complaining. It was just funny."

Nina gave me a sideways glance, but I was busy trying to act innocent. "Uh, who—who was doing it?"

Trent laughed again. "I don't know. I guess she found someone else to bake for. Too bad, though. I miss those cookies. And it was cool, you know? A surprise." He munched on another cookie. "These taste like those cookies." He raised his eyebrows, grinning. "Want my locker combination?"

I didn't have time to come up with a witty comeback (as if I could). Just then Caitlin breezed up to us. "Trent, can I talk to you for a second, alone?"

"Sure," he said. "Do you want a cookie? Megan made them for me. They're really good." He put his arm around me, making no move to do as Caitlin requested—talk with her alone. "Do you know Megan? Megan this is Caitlin. We used to date."

"But now I date Shane Franks," Caitlin told him curtly. "And I hear you're dating Megan the Mormon, here. Actually, that's what I wanted to talk to you about. Is it true? Because I don't believe it."

Trent shrugged. "We're going to the dance together."

Caitlin eyed him incredulously. "You're really going to a school dance?" The information seemed impossible for her to choke down.

He nodded. "I really am." Then he added, "With Megan."

Caitlin glanced over at me, giving me such a look of contempt I was afraid I had a booger hanging out of my nose. What was with her? She didn't even know me. How could I possibly bug her so much?

"I don't believe this," Caitlin said. "What are you planning on doing with her after the dance? Have milk and cookies?"

Trent shrugged, taking another bite of his cookie. "Yeah, maybe. These are really good."

Scowling at him, Caitlin opened her mouth as though she was going to say something else. Only she didn't. Instead, she stalked away.

I watched her storm off, still dazed by her open hostility. "Well, I guess the deal's working," I said. "Your taking me to the dance really seems to bug her."

Trent grinned. "Told you." He took another cookie. "But what about you and Conner? Are you sure you want him back?"

The way he asked the question, it was as though he was certain our deal would work and that Conner would come crawling back to me. He made it sound as though whether Conner and I reunited or not would be my decision. Which was crazy, but I answered him truthfully anyway, since he seemed to want the truth. "I don't know."

There was a time, not long ago, the answer would have been a definite, desperate, "Yes." But now I wasn't so sure. My heart wanted him back. My heart ached for him. But my head told me, "No. Megan, he cheated on you. He lied to you. He *dumped* you. You deserve better." And sometimes I was strong enough to listen to my head instead of my wimpy heart. Sometimes . . . just not very often.

chapter 8

Every day for the rest of the week, Trent ate lunch with Nina and me. Obviously, it was to stir up Caitlin and Conner, and work the deal. But it was cool having him around. He was a nice guy—and funny. (And cute and adorable and . . .) I had to keep reminding myself he was all wrong for me, and that his affectionate attention was simply an act, but it was hard. He was a good actor and I was a sap.

Friday during lunch, Caitlin came up to us again. "So, you kids having fun?" she asked, sounding as though we were toddlers playing in a sandbox. "Enjoying your little prayer meeting?" She ditched her cheerful act, scowling at Trent. "What are you *doing* with these losers, Trent?"

Trent stood up. "Watch who you call losers. Megan's really sweet. She's nothing like you."

Caitlin shot him daggers with her eyes. "You're unbelievable."

Trent shook his head. "No. You're unbelievable. You want to date a drug dealer? I can't stop you. Go ahead and make stupid choices. But don't put Megan down for making the right ones."

Again, Caitlin shot him daggers. She said a curse word under her breath as she stormed away. We all watched her go in silence. Finally, I asked sadly, "She's getting into drugs?"

Trent ran his hands through his hair, looking sort of miserable. "Caitlin's into 'recreational stuff' as she puts it. But you know, stuff like that, it just gets worse." Trent studied me. "Well, I guess maybe you don't know, but it does."

I bit my lip, feeling sad. Poor Caitlin. I knew she despised me, but I couldn't help feeling sorry for her. It was weird. People got on unexpected paths. "Sometimes life is really hard," I murmured.

"Yeah," Nina said reflectively. "Just like your song."

Trent's eyes lit up with interest. "What song?"

"Oh. It's nothing," I said, embarrassed. He was in a band. He was excited because he thought Nina was talking about *his* kind of music, that kind of song. "It's for church."

"It's *not* nothing," Nina protested. "Megan writes beautiful songs. And we're singing one of them in church this Sunday. Megan has a solo."

I kicked her under the table. Nina only laughed. "What? It's true. And what are you afraid of anyway? That he's going to come to church and hear you?"

Trent surprised her by saying, "I am."

I choked on the water I was drinking, almost keeling over.

"What?" I gasped.

Trent raised his eyebrows, looking serious. "I'm going to come hear you sing."

Trent Ryan was planning to come to our church? I couldn't believe it. I could barely drag Conner to church most Sundays when we were dating and he was a member—and my boyfriend. What was up with Trent? Caitlin wasn't the only one baffled by this new side of him. I was too. Apparently, so was Nina.

She wouldn't shut up about how romantic it was that Trent was coming to hear my song. Once Trent left, for the rest of lunch, she gushed on and on about it. "First he saves you from Aspen's wicked attempt to humiliate you, then he defends you against Caitlin who supposedly broke his heart, and now he's going to church to hear you sing." Nina beamed. "Trent Ryan is going to *church* for you."

"Not for me," I pointed out. "Nina, the guy is in a band. He's Mr. Music."

"So," Nina was still beaming, "you're *Miss* Music. The two of you are the perfect couple. You can make beautiful music together."

I bit my lip, wishing that was true. But it wasn't.

"Nina, we don't do the same *kind* of music. Trent is going to come to church and laugh at me."

"No he's not." Nina sounded so sure of herself that I almost believed her. I *wanted* to believe her, that was for sure. "Your song is beautiful, Megan."

I threw away the rest of my lunch, knowing Nina was right. My song was beautiful. My little brother, Brent, inspired it. He died five years ago of leukemia. The pain of losing him still ran incredibly deep. The song was about how hard life can be sometimes, but how I can still feel Brent near me, and that I know I'll see him again—on the road home.

My song *was* beautiful. But it wasn't Trent's kind of song.

* * * * *

I sat in Language Arts, trying to concentrate on *Beowulf*, but nothing would sink in. Nothing but, *Trent is coming to church?*

Even if he meant it at the time (because I had to admit, he did look as though he meant it) I was positive he wouldn't show on Sunday. He would talk himself out of it. After all, this was Trent Ryan we were talking about. He had a reputation as a party animal to protect. Then again, he didn't seem that interested in protecting it. After all, he was letting the whole school think he had a romantic interest in me, Megan the Mormon. And he was taking me to the dance.

But that would all end tomorrow. Tomorrow *was* the dance. Then the deal would be over. He wouldn't have to act interested in me anymore. There would be no reason for him to come to church.

I sighed, kinda sad. Tomorrow it would all be over. Tomorrow night at the stroke of twelve, no more ball. No more Prince. The spell would be broken. I'd be a pumpkin again.

"Oh well," I sighed.

It had been fun getting such devoted attention from Trent. But, despite the fact I'd miss his fake-but-oh-so-realistic affection, and the tormented state it put Conner in. Even with that—I'd be relieved when the dance was over. Trent did strange, mystical things to my heart. And he could break it so easily, even with my knowledge that we were only putting on a show. Because the thing was—it didn't always feel like a show. Not to me. As I said, he was a good actor and I was a sap.

"Only one more day to get through," I told myself. "I can hold it together for that."

But just then, there was an announcement over the intercom. "Due to circumstances beyond our control, the spring dance has been rescheduled for two weeks from Saturday."

I groaned. Two weeks! No! My heart couldn't take it. It couldn't! It was already wavering. Two weeks and it would be pudding.

Besides, Trent wouldn't last. He couldn't. I'd seen him dump girls in shorter time. Plenty of them. And he'd been interested in those girls for real. How could I possibly hold his attention for that long when all of this was only pretend?

I was doomed.

chapter 9

Right after class, I spotted Raven at her locker. All week long, she had been giving me dirty looks. And all week long, I'd been ignoring them because I didn't know what to say or do. As I've mentioned before, I'm not into drama scenes. And having to say, "Hey, calm down, I'm not after your boyfriend," seemed kind of drama-ish.

I'd thought about writing her a note. One I could mail to her or leave in her locker. One that would spare me a face-to-face confrontation. But I thought the direct approach might work better. Since every time I tried to write her a note, I'd end up staring at a blank page for an hour. Because that was it, when it came to dealing with this kind of stuff, my mind was a blank. What was I supposed to do? I had exactly no clue, but I needed Brian. And I sure didn't need another enemy. So, I knew I needed to do something.

And suddenly, here was Raven, right in front of me, at her locker. It was like a neon sign flashing, "Time for that something."

So, I took a deep breath and walked over to her and I started talking before I could talk myself out of it or actually *think* about what I was doing.

"Hey, Raven," I said hastily, getting right to the point, "I think there's some sort of misunderstanding between us."

Raven put her hands on her hips, saying nothing, but looking ultra-menacing. I took a step back. Suddenly, I knew I'd made a big mistake. Shoulda gone with the note thing. I knew it!

"I, uh . . . that is, Brian and I, we're just practicing for the duet together. That's it. Nothing more. I mean, I'm not trying to steal him away or anything."

"Right," she said, but it sounded more like she was saying, "Yes you are."

"Seriously," I said. "I don't want any problems. I just really want to win the competition—"

"And my boyfriend," she interjected. "You think I'm stupid?"

Dumbstruck, I shook my head.

"Look, just because Brian and I are having troubles right now, you think you can make up some lame excuse about a stupid duet and wiggle in between us? Well, it won't work. Just keep your lame excuses and your stupid cookies to yourself, or I'll *give* you a problem."

Whoa!

I watched her storm away, choking on the fact that she'd just threatened me.

"That went well," I muttered.

"What went well?"

I whipped around to find Trent standing behind me.

"Uh, nothing."

He grinned, like I was a cute little kid. "Anyway, did you hear that announcement about the dance? That they've moved it to the eighth?"

"Yeah," I said, knowing this was the part where he backed out. Commitment: everyone knew he choked on it. I mean, the guy dumped our *Homecoming Queen* before a month passed. And she'd even let him ditch the homecoming dance. The guy had issues. "It's okay if you don't want to go through with it," I told him. "I understand."

He furrowed his brow. "Are you backing out?"

"No. I just thought—no, I'm not backing out."

He smiled. "Good. I'll see ya Sunday."

His words hit me like a bolt of lightning. But he was gone, swallowed up into the crowded hall of students. *I'll see ya Sunday?* See ya Sunday!!!! He really was coming to church?

* * * * *

After school, I had to make up a test I'd missed last week in calculus. When I got to Mr. Bank's class, he wasn't there yet. But a group of students were waiting in his classroom. One of them was Conner.

"Hey," he smiled when he saw me come in and my heart kind of melted.

I took the closest seat I could grab, because suddenly my legs were shaky. This was how I got when I chanced to see Conner unexpectedly, I was a mess.

Conner came over and took a seat beside me.

"Here to take a make-up test?"

I nodded, wondering who helped him study for calculus now. Laura? I didn't think she was even in calculus. But maybe he went to the tutor lab. It was weird, and sort of painful, not knowing what was going on in his life.

"You'll love this," Conner said with a grin. He started telling me a funny story about his five-year-old brother Dillon. How he's been preparing for a talk in primary on the "Holy Goat."

I listened with a dull pain. It hurt to be sitting with him, talking with him, yet unable to touch him. When would I get used to it? When would the pain go away?

The door opened and I turned, expecting it to be Mr. Banks, but it wasn't. It was Laura. She glared at me, then turned her gaze to Conner. "Can I talk to you for a second?"

Conner furrowed his brow. "Sure."

He got up and followed her out of the class. He didn't come back.

chapter 10

On Sunday before sacrament meeting I kept looking around for Trent. But I didn't really, truly expect him to show. No way. Trent Ryan here at church? The image was impossible to conjure up. Despite my discovering what a nice guy he was, Trent had a sort of bad-boy reputation. And though I knew better than to believe most of the rumors I heard around school, I knew some of them were grounded in at least a little bit of reality. After all, Trent was a partier.

Besides, I was fairly certain he was only teasing me Friday when he said he would come. Only, he had looked completely serious.

But this was Trent Ryan we were talking about. *Trent Ryan*. He didn't go to school dances, and he didn't go to church.

But then again, he was taking me to the dance, wasn't he? Realizing that made me smile. Why was he breaking one of his rules for me? Just then my heart caught in my throat, because right in the middle of the opening hymn, *in walked Trent*.

He was wearing a suit and looking adorable, and standing beside him was Wendy. They both took seats in the folding chairs back in the overflow. Trent saw me and waved. Then he pointed me out to Wendy and her face lit up as she waved to me too—very enthusiastically. I waved back, so excited to see them both at church, I didn't even think to be nervous about the fact that they were going to hear me sing.

I sat through the announcements, and then listened to the talks with more attention than I ever paid in my entire life, trying to hear them as Trent would, as a non-member. What would he think of terms like "eternal mate" and "temple marriage"? Would he think we were nuts for believing families can be together forever?

When the bishop announced that it was now time for a special musical number by the Laurels, I shot up as though waking from a dream. *Oh yeah*, I thought with alarm, I'm singing. It was shocking that I had been able to forget about that. I'm a good singer. I sing all the time. But that reassurance had never stopped me from being nervous. I was amazed that Trent's showing up at church had occupied so much of my brain that I didn't have room in it to worry about my performance. What did that say?

We Laurels stood around the piano and Sister Woodland played the intro and then we were singing. Normally I would stare at the wall ahead, hoping I appeared as though I was looking out into the congregation. But today I looked at Wendy. Her beaming face didn't make me nervous. Her happy smile filled me with confidence. When it was time to sing my solo, I sang it to her.

When the meeting was over, Trent brought Wendy over to me. She gave me a big hug. "You sing beautifully," she said, hugging me again. "Look, I brought your Wendy poem." She showed me the silly poem I had written her at the beginning of the school year. "I keep it on my wall, over my bed," she said. "Can you autograph it for me?"

I laughed. "Sure."

She gave me a purple pen and I wrote, "To my favorite camper, Wendy. Love, Piglet (Megan Turner)." I should maybe explain that. My camp name was Piglet.

I'm sure I could have come up with something more eloquent to write to Wendy if I'd had more time (like an hour) but Trent was standing there gazing at me sorta enamored, and that was turning my brain sort of mushy. So I felt I was lucky to eek out even that tiny morsel of wit, since at the moment I was finding it difficult to remember the spelling of my own name.

Wendy read my message and laughed.

"Thanks Piglet," she said.

"You should be in a band," Trent said, and that was the first time I actually dared look at him since I waved when he first came in. He stared into my eyes. "I knew you could write songs," he said, and then added quickly, "uh, because Wendy told me. But I had no idea you could sing like that."

"She's a Madrigal at school," Nina piped in.

Trent looked at her quizzically. "A what?"

Nina dropped her jaw, faking injury. "You don't know about Madrigals? It's the honor choir at our school and it's a great *honor* to be in it."

Nina was in it too. I probably should have pointed that out, but instead I just swooned at the way Trent was gazing at me.

He didn't seem to know what to do with the Madrigals information, though. Finally, he seemed to simply dismiss it. "Anyway, you're a good singer," he said.

That meant so much to me, not just because I had a huge, stupid, monster crush on him, but also because he himself was a singer.

"Thanks," I whispered.

We stood looking at each other. To me it was a magical moment full of unsaid feelings of deep affection. But maybe for him it was just an awkward pause in the conversation.

When he spoke, he surprised me by asking, "So, there's Sunday school classes now?"

I widened my eyes with surprise. "Yeah. Do you want to stay?"

"Yeah. I was kind of interested," he said. "But could I go into Wendy's class with her? She's kind of shy."

"Sure," I said, maybe a little too eagerly. I was just so stunned and thrilled he was going to stay. I led them over to Sister Springsteed, the Valiant 10 teacher, introducing them with pride.

"Well," Sister Springsteed beamed, "we're thrilled to have you with us. Come on and I'll introduce you to the class." She led them off to the adventure of primary, and I watched them go, glad they were in such capable hands. I hadn't thought to warn Trent that he was in for another two hours of church. But Sister Springsteed was fun and spiritual. She would make class meaningful, and I knew Wendy would like sharing time with all the singing. So, I skipped off to Sunday school floating on a cloud of happiness.

But when I got to class, Conner was there, looking solemn. "Can I talk to you for a minute?"

I swallowed. "Sure."

We went out into the hall.

"Why are you doing this?" he asked.

I widened my eyes, having no idea what he was talking about. "Doing what?"

"Hanging out with Trent. Megan," he said earnestly, "you're making a mistake. You're a sweet girl. I don't want to see you get hurt."

I swallowed, unable to say anything. *He* had hurt me.

Conner went on, "Look, I had to go in and talk to the bishop this afternoon. I can't even take the sacrament right now."

"Oh."

"I don't want you getting messed up in anything like I did—and I can't believe you would be interested in a guy like that anyway. Megan, he's only interested in one thing."

That made me gaze up at him. "What? Coming to church? Sorry, Conner. I don't see that as a problem." I started to walk away, but he grabbed my arm.

"You called me Conner," he said, sounding hurt.

I didn't know what to say, "You're not Cody to me anymore"? I couldn't get the words out. But I didn't call him Conner to hurt him. Or did I?

Conner bit his lip. "Anyway, you sang really beautiful. You looked ... beautiful."

I could feel tears forming in my eyes. "I—I have to go."

I hurried to the bathroom where I could cry in peace. And I did. I sobbed and sobbed. What was Conner trying to do to me? He broke my heart over and over.

It hadn't just been the break up. The pain had started before that. He'd made me feel stupid for worrying about him spending so much time with Laura. He'd kept insisting, "Laura and I are only lab partners. I'm only helping her study." I knew that wasn't all they were doing, but what could I say? He kept denying it. Then one day, out of the blue, he said, "Maybe we should spend a little time apart." And the very next day—the next *day*!—he showed up at school holding hands with Laura.

I shouldn't let him get to me now, I told myself. I should be an Ice Queen.

chapter 11

Tonight I stayed up practically all night writing in my journal, which happens to be my laptop computer. I lay in bed and typed away at top speed, ignoring the spell checker, just typing anything and everything that came into my mind. I had so many thoughts and questions and hopes about both Trent and Conner and I just typed them as they came to me, crying sometimes. But always typing. Typing, typing, typing.

What has gotten into Trent? He didn't only come to church, which in itself is pretty much a miracle. But he also stayed for the whole three hours. Why? Why would he do that? I could understand if he knew anything about our religion. Anything. But as far as I know, I'm the only Mormon he's ever associated with in his life. And he only started to get to know me this week.

And another thing about that: Why does he act as though he knows me? Why?!!! Telling Aspen that he didn't go to a school dance before because until now he hadn't met the "right girl." And why did he say Conner would want me back once he realized what a "great girl" he lost? And why did he tell Caitlin I was "good and sweet"? What makes

> him think he knows me? And what made him say all of those things? Just to irritate Aspen? Just to make Caitlin mad?
>
> And why is he breaking all of his rules? Why is he taking me, of all people, to the dance? He never took any of his girlfriends, and they were, well, his girlfriends. And they were all popular and beautiful, and his type. I'm none of those things. I'm just me.
>
> And what's up with Conner? He had to go see the bishop? And he can't take the sacrament? I'm not sure what that even means, exactly. I guess he and Laura . . . I don't know. I don't even want to think about it, but it's making me cry. I can't believe how much he's changed in just two months. Two months! But

The words stopped appearing on my screen. Grrr! My computer crashed, again!

"Hunk of junk," I grumbled as I put my laptop away and crawled back into bed.

Just the other night my computer had crashed while I was in the middle of an English paper. I had to redo tons of my work because I'm not much of a saver. As I'm in the throes of writing, I don't think about saving. I just let my fingers work magic. That had been fine with my old computer. It had been slow, but reliable. Unfortunately, I'd let Conner talk me into selling it.

"This thing's ancient," he would always complain. "You could pick up something way faster on eBay."

Finally, he wore me down. I sold my trusty Mac, my friend.

Conner helped me choose a laptop off eBay Local, so I could pick it up without having to pay for shipping. He promised that my new computer would be way faster. And it was. It was super quick. The only problem was, it was also super quick to crash.

"I'm going to sell it," I told myself before drifting off to sleep. No need to keep Conner mistakes lingering around, tormenting me.

I even knew where I could get a new Mac. Nina's brother was leaving on his mission soon and eager to sell his. Yay for me!

The next morning, I put my laptop up for sale on eBay before leaving for seminary. And three days later it was sold for a nice price, considering. But when I told Trent my happy news at lunch, he didn't seem happy for me. He seemed concerned.

"It's no big deal," I told him. "I sold my other computer on eBay. Everything was fine."

That didn't appease Trent. He still seemed concerned. "Did you already send it?"

I polished off my pizza. "No. I didn't sell it locally this time. I have to box it up."

Trent bit his lip. "Megan, make sure you clear your hard-drive." The way he said it, it was like a big-serious deal to him. I thought it was incredibly sweet he was so concerned for me.

"I will."

He looked at me questioningly. "Did you clear your other one?"

"Yeah—well, *I* didn't. But Conner did."

"I'll clear it, okay?" Trent said. "I'll clear it for you."

I nodded. "Sure. If you want to. It's a big deal, huh?"

I didn't see how it could be, though. I didn't keep anything on it that could be used for identity fraud. No social security or bank account numbers. Nothing like that. Just schoolwork and poems and songs I was working on, and sad, pathetic journal entries. Nothing that would interest anyone but me. Sure, I would be embarrassed if someone read my stuff. I'd die. But I doubted I could *pay* someone to actually sit down and read it, let alone worry they would seek it out.

But if he wanted to clear my hard drive, I sure wasn't going to stop him. He could clear away.

"I'll come over right after school," he said.

I smiled. "Okay."

He was coming over. That couldn't be shrugged off as a ploy to make the dance date "look real." There would be no Caitlin or Conner or anyone around to put on a show for. It seemed Trent Ryan was really and truly my friend. He was going to clear my hard-drive for me. Wasn't that proof?

I was glad I had already transferred all of my old hard-drive information over to my new computer. I didn't want Trent to have to do anything where he might actually see anything I wrote—since my computer was full of stuff about him.

$$* \quad * \quad * \quad * \quad *$$

When Trent came over I was in the midst of making cookies for the blood drive our school was hosting tomorrow afternoon.

"I'm almost done," I told him as Mom led him into the kitchen.

He looked surprised when he saw our kitchen full of cookies. "Are all these for me?" he asked with a grin.

I laughed. "Help yourself, but they're for the blood drive tomorrow. Everyone gets a cookie after they give blood. It's to elevate their blood-sugar level, or something."

Trent gazed at me thoughtfully. "You're always volunteering, huh?"

I blushed at the way he stared. "I just wanted to help and I can't donate blood."

Trent raised an eyebrow. "Why?"

My blush went a few shades deeper. I didn't want to admit I'm a runt.

"You have to meet a certain weight requirement," I explained, and then quickly went on, hoping he didn't have time to digest that I'm too scrawny to donate a little blood. "But I wanted to help. So," I gestured around the kitchen, "cookies."

Trent munched on a peanut butter one, still gazing at me. "You're always doing good," he said.

Why'd he say that? Why did he act as though he knew me so well? And was it supposed to be some sort of slam? After all, he said

I bugged Caitlin by being "Miss Goodness and Light." Did I bug him too? It didn't *seem* like it. And he didn't seem to be making fun of me. But was he? Was I just too naive to see it?

Nothing was clear.

The way he was looking at me made it seem as though I was the most beautiful, special, wonderful girl that ever walked the planet. But why would he look at me that way? He didn't know me. Not really. Not well enough to see past my lack of "obvious" beauty. The kind that Caitlin and Aspen possessed. That's the kind you stare at. And that's the kind of girls he was used to dating.

I tried to look away from him, tried to get a grip. He was only teasing, right? That had to be it. He seemed to like to make me blush.

But all I accomplished by trying to keep my composure was backing into the kitchen counter. Ouch!

"I'll, uh, get my computer," I told him and zoomed out of the room like a spaz on steroids.

* * * * *

Once Trent finished clearing my hard drive, Seth and I taught him "Killer Uno." It's actually just normal Uno, but my family—being the game players that we are—added extra rules to make the game more exciting. Mom and Seth's friend, Kevin, joined in as well. So, we had a little party—the Mormon kind—with Kool-Aid and cookies and green Jell-O. Though, I'm just kidding about the Jell-O. We had fish sticks.

When it was time for Trent to leave, I walked him to the door. "Thanks for clearing my hard drive."

He grinned. "Yeah, well, thanks for stomping all over me in Uno."

The way he said that made me laugh. "Hey, anytime."

He stared at me a moment. "I like your laugh."

"I like yours too."

Doh!

His eyes twinkled, but he didn't mention my dorkyness. Instead he grinned, saying he'd see me tomorrow.

I watched him drive away. Then I ran up to my room to do a little dance. He liked my laugh!

chapter 12

I work at the mall in a department store called Jordon's. It's a good job. I like it. I just don't get a lot of money working there. It's not that they don't pay me well. They do, I guess. I just don't get to put in a lot of hours. So, I can't, of course, expect a big, fat paycheck. But I do get a thirty percent discount on everything in the store. That helps. Plus, the store has a petite section. So, it's been nice. These days I actually fit in my clothes. And it's made a difference. Seriously. I actually get compliments sometimes instead of "scrawny" jokes.

Tonight during a major lull at work, I tried on an elegant satin wrap from the morning's shipment. I stood in front of the evening section's full-length mirror, admiring myself in it, thinking how perfect it would be for the dance. It was just for fun, though. No way could I afford it. But wow, if I could . . .

I posed.

Then I pretended I was Trent at the dance, admiring me in it. "You look stunning," I/Trent told my image in the mirror.

But then—this is so embarrassing!—suddenly there was Trent, standing behind me. For real! I could see him in the mirror, grinning. My face turned so red, it was purple.

"You really do look stunning," he agreed, his eyes twinkling with amusement.

"Thank you." I did a little curtsy, trying to act as though I wasn't about to die of embarrassment.

Finishing my performance, I swooped the wrap off in record speed, placing it back on the display. Then I tried to act calm. Composed. Semi-normal. "What are you doing here?"

"I was in the mall," he said. "I thought I'd drop by and say hi."

I'm sure my face gave away how thrilled I was that he thought to do that. Maybe that's why he said the next thing.

"Are you going to be off pretty soon?" he asked. "I want you to hear my band."

"Uh, tonight?"

"Yeah. There's no school tomorrow. Saturday, remember?"

"Yeah, but . . ."

"It's not at a party," he said quickly, seeming to understand my hesitation. "It's at Flips. So no drinking or anything. Totally Mormon friendly."

Flips was a new pizza place. But it was more than just a pizza place. It was our school's hangout. Think Chuck E. Cheese, but for teenagers, and instead of mechanical animals on stage, think cool bands. That was Flips.

What was extra cool was the bands didn't only play there, they worked there too. They waited tables and bused and, you know, "worked." That's how Flips paid them, for their work, not their performance. But we teens, we definitely came for the performances. Although the pizza was seriously good too.

"We're dead tonight," I told him. "I can get off now. Only, I don't have my car. My mom was going to pick me up."

"I can give you a ride," Trent offered. Then he raised an eyebrow. "If you're not afraid of my driving."

I called Mom and she said it would be okay, although she seemed a little hesitant. "Do you really have to stay out so late?"

"Well, the place closes at twelve," I explained. "And Trent has to clean up before he can lock up."

Mom consented. Lucky for me, she hated seeing me mope around the house, picking at my Conner wounds. Also, Mom liked Trent. She thought it was sweet that he was so protective of Wendy. And she was a lot like Nina. She thought it was romantic that Trent had rescued me from Aspen's torment that day in class.

At Flips, I had a blast. It was fun walking in with Trent, having people glance up from their conversations and stare. They were beginning to really believe we were a couple. Imagine it, Megan The Mormon and Trent The Party Guy, a pair.

No way!

Trent bought me a soda and we played air hockey and I beat him in skee-ball and I was having a blast. But then it was time for Trent to go backstage and set up with his band. None of my friends were around. Suddenly, I felt anxious, as though I was being abandoned in a foreign country.

I was going to be alone. That wouldn't have been so bad. I definitely could have dealt with it, alone. Only did it have to be in front of every cool person from school?

Trent got me settled into a table up front. "Don't leave," he said before going backstage, seeming to notice my anxiety. "Seriously, I really want you to hear us."

"I won't leave," I promised.

Then I sat alone with my root beer, playing with the straw. Trent had hooked me up with a great table. I didn't want to lose it. It was right near the stage. But I felt conspicuous being all alone. How long would I have to sit here before the show started?

"Hey, Megan, can we sit with you?"

I looked up to see Brooke Hunter and a group of her friends.

"Sure," I said, probably a bit over-eagerly. I didn't really know Brooke all that well, and I sure didn't know her friends, but I was elated I wouldn't have to sit alone any longer.

"This is a great table," Brooke said with a smile. "We usually have to sit in the back. Is Baggage playing tonight?"

It was weird. Brooke asked about them as though I was an authority on Trent and his band. I played along, having fun. Why not? It wasn't everyday I was assumed the-one-to-know about a cool, hot guy and his band. "Yep," I said, real casual-like. "Baggage is playing."

There were two other bands that played first. They both only played a few songs, though. Baggage was the main event.

When Trent came out on stage my heart did some sort of weird flip thing. He gave me a smile, and in return I blushed bright red for him, and gave him a big, dopey grin the size of Texas. Baggage played their most popular songs first. It was cool. I felt proud, as though Trent really was my boyfriend. Okay, I knew he wasn't, but no one else did. As unlikely as it seemed, everyone believed the hot guy on the stage was my true "significant other."

Once everyone finally stopped applauding, Trent made an announcement. "This next song is really special. And a really special person wrote it. She's sitting at that table right over there." Trent pointed at *my* table.

I stared at him in bewilderment. What was he *talking* about?

Trent only smiled.

Boy, he had a great smile, but my stomach knotted. What was going on?

The music started. It was my song, *The Road Home*. Trent's band was playing my song! Whoa! And it was *beautiful*. I sat motionless, stunned. Through the whole thing, I didn't breathe. I just sat, listening.

When it was over everyone stood, applauding. Hordes of people, cool people from school, came up to me, gushing about my song. Telling me how beautiful it was. How romantic it was. How it made them cry. And then, Trent was there, beside me. "I hope you don't mind," he said. "Us playing your song."

"No, I don't mind." I hugged him, because that's what I do when I'm excited. I hug. But once I had him in my arms, I woke to reality. I was hugging Trent Ryan.

"It was beautiful," I told him, quickly pulling away.

"Well, it would have been better with you up there on stage," Trent said. "You should have been the one singing it."

"No way!" I protested. "You were awesome! Amazing!" I had to fight the urge to hug him again. But as it was, we were still standing really close from the hug I'd just given him, and although there were still gobs of admirers surrounding us, for a moment, it was as though we were alone. Just the two of us. Trent and me.

Magic.

Trent took a step back and said, "I better get busy."

I sat for a while with Brooke and her friends, eating up their compliments and everyone else's. It was incredibly thrilling, though everyone was confused and thought *The Road Home* was a love song, about the death of a boyfriend, not my brother. But, hey, that was okay. It was great to have fans—and confused fans were better than no fans.

So, I was having a terrific time. But, all I really wanted to do was rush home and bake Trent cookies. A giant locker's worth.

* * * * *

Once everyone had gone home, I helped clean up. Then Trent sat with his guitar, and strummed my song. "Sing it," he said. "Up here, on stage."

I shook my head, feeling shy. But then without even realizing I was going to, I got up there and started singing anyway. I wanted to. Needed to. Hearing the music made me want to sing, and it was fun to grab the mike and belt it loud and strong, and move to the music up on stage.

I glanced over at Trent and he was smiling as though he was really pleased. He seemed to be having as much fun as me, so I went on singing and dancing to the dim, empty room, having the time of my life.

"You should do that for a real audience," Trent said on the way home.

"Oh. I couldn't," I told him, and then laughed. "I don't know if you know this, but I'm shy."

He grinned. "I hadn't noticed."

I besieged him with questions about my song. How did he know the words? How did his band learn the song so fast?

Trent surprised me by pulling off to the side of the road. It made me grip the door handle with alarm. What was he *doing*?

"Sorry, I didn't mean to scare you," he said, sensing my panic. "I just wanted to talk to you for a minute." He was silent a moment, then went on, choosing his words with care. "Your song, it's sort of like you explain the unexplainable. At least it had always been unexplainable to me. Only now, I don't know. Your song, it touched me. It's comforting."

I sat back in my seat, unable to speak for fear of crying. His words touched *me*. They were the sweetest, kindest words I had ever heard in my entire life. And the most amazing part was—they'd come from Trent Ryan.

When I didn't say anything, Trent went on. "I couldn't get your song out of my head. And when I played it for the guys, they got into it. We played it, like, all day every day for the past week."

Hearing that filled me with excitement. Baggage was the coolest band around. And they liked my song! And to have heard it played by them, and better yet, sung by Trent, this was like, the best night of my life!

chapter 13

On Sunday I had car trouble and got to church late. But, hey, I got there, a little oily smelling, but no holes in my nylons, so I considered myself lucky.

As I was standing in the chapel doorway, scanning the congregation for my family, my heart sped up about a thousand beats per second because guess who was there, again? Trent and Wendy! They were sitting in the overflow. When I saw them, I about tripped over a chair. (Graceful entrances aren't exactly my thing.)

I wanted to go sit with them. I really, really wanted to sit with them. But I couldn't get my stupid, almost-tripping-over-a-chair feet to move in their direction. Instead, the cowards scurried over to sit with my parents.

It was testimony meeting, and the whole hour was jam packed with spirituality. I couldn't have asked for a better meeting if I had prepared it myself, telling the congregation, "Okay guys, make it super tear-jerky. This is for my pretend boyfriend." I kept wanting to look back to see how Trent was doing, what he thought of the spiritual fest. But I didn't look back, not once. Well, okay, once.

It was when Conner got up on the stand to bear his testimony, which I'd never seen him do before in my life. He actually *bore his testimony.* Only, I got the feeling he was up there more just to prove a point. Because it was mostly about the pitfalls of dating non-members. And at one point he looked straight at me, saying, "Sometimes you just don't know what you've got until you don't have it any more. Then you realize how special it is."

My heart started pounding like crazy. Thump, thump, thump.

And he was staring at me in church, from the pulpit. That's not allowed, is it? It's like a rule or something. What was he trying to do to me?

I had to look away. I glanced back at Trent. He raised his eyebrows, like "I told you so."

But after traumatizing me, Conner went on to talk about the church. "It's special," he said, "you may not even realize how special until it's not in your life anymore."

This wasn't like Conner, coming to church two Sundays in a row, let alone bearing his testimony. I hadn't even been sure he *had* a testimony. He'd always said, "Yours is strong enough for both of us, Megan."

Either he had really changed, or he was up there for all the wrong reasons. And I had the sinking feeling it was the latter. He was proving a point. It made me feel funny, but I hoped I was wrong. I hoped he was up there being honest. I hoped he really had gained a testimony.

After the meeting, Conner came up to me before I could get to Trent. "I have to go to work," Conner said. "So I can't stay. But I hope you understood what I was trying to say up there."

I looked at him quizzically, saying nothing. I *didn't* understand. Did he bear his testimony, or try to woo me? And if it was the wooing, which I got the feeling it was, what brought it on? Seeing that Trent had come to church? Seeing that Conner might actually lose me as his little loyal puppy dog? The one that wagged its tail any time he gave it the tiniest bit of attention, even after it had been kicked around and rejected by him?

I knew I should be an Ice Queen to him. I knew I should be cold, contemptuous. After all, he had hurt me. Hurt me so, so, so bad. But the way he gazed at me melted my heart.

"Look, we need talk," he said. "I'll call you later."

"Uh . . . okay."

And then he was gone, out of the church. And I was left wondering, what just happened? I had a strange, excited pang in my heart or stomach or . . . somewhere. But I knew I was being stupid.

Stupid, stupid, stupid. *Don't get excited for his call!* I scolded myself. He dumped you. He hurt you. Don't be a puppy dog. Be an Ice Queen.

But I didn't feel like an Ice Queen.

When I found Trent, he was already out in the hall. "You came!" I told him excitedly.

"Yeah," he smiled at my excitement. "Sister Springsteed gave Wendy an assignment last week. A scripture to study and talk about in class today. And, well, Wendy wanted to come and do the assignment."

"Oh." I should have known. He'd come for Wendy. But that didn't change anything. I was still thrilled that he came.

Trent grinned, looking sheepish. "I have an assignment too."

That made me laugh. It was so sweet, to think of him, Trent Ryan, sharing a scripture with his classmates, a pack of ten-year-olds. I wished I could be there.

"So, your boyfriend seems to want you back," Trent said, putting his hands in his front pockets. "But are you sure you want him back? Megan, you're too good for that guy."

chapter 14

All day Sunday I waited for a call that never came. And I was so pathetic, spending the entire day wondering what I was going to tell Conner. Would I forgive him? Would I take him back? He'd have to actually beg me, I'd told myself.

And then he never called.

Hmm.

Monday, I saw him at his locker, with Laura. And the pain hurt all over again. What kind of game was he playing? I didn't know. Didn't understand. But I didn't want any part of it. It hurt too much.

"Jerk!" I muttered under my breath, fighting back tears.

Just then I noticed Aspen watching me from her group of friends. She had her usual wicked smirk on her face. I turned away, like I hadn't noticed.

No way was I going to let her see me cry. I started gabbing animatedly with three Madrigals nearby. I laughed hysterically with them, as though I didn't have a care in the world, as though I didn't have a knife in my back.

* * * * *

Tuesday was even worse, because I actually ran right into Conner and Laura. Literally. They were coming out of the library as I was going in. Conner accidentally smacked me in the head with the door.

"Oh, Megan, geez, I'm sorry," he said, sounding truly contrite.

For what? I wondered. For hitting me with the door or being a jerk?

59

He helped me to a bench, and then examined my head. "You're going to have a bump."

Oh good, I thought, still seeing stars. That'll look pretty for the dance.

At least now I'd actually have a physical wound, one that could be seen. For once, visual evidence of the pain Conner caused me.

"She's fine," Laura said, seeming angry at the way Conner was fussing over me. He was being . . . tender. "Come on. We're going to be late."

"You go ahead," Conner said. "I'm going to take her to the nurse."

Laura put her hands on her hips, looking ready to explode. She opened her mouth as though she was going to protest, loudly. But then she didn't. Instead she huffed away.

I told Conner I didn't want to go to the nurse, I just wanted to get to class.

Conner tried talking me out of it, saying I could have a concussion. "I'll just walk you to the nurse's office," he said. "She should look at you, Megan. Just to make sure you're alright."

When his cajoling didn't work, he sighed. "Wait here."

He bought a soda from the vending machine.

I blinked.

Did he think he could buy me off with a soda? Well, I was kind of thirsty. But then, he didn't even offer it to me. Instead he placed the cold can on my injured head.

"The coldness should keep down the swelling," he said, still looking concerned.

He was being so kind and doing that tender thing. It was nice. But actually, it made me feel like crying. Why did I still like him so much? Why? Why couldn't I just *stop* liking him?

"Remember that morning we hiked up to the peak to watch the sunrise?" he said softly.

I nodded, feeling tears rush to my eyes. Why did he have to bring *that* up? Why now? It sure wasn't going to help me stop liking him. Far from it. It was only going to rip out my heart. Tear it to shreds.

That day had been great. Magical. We had packed a breakfast and ate it at the top of the mountain. We had stayed up there all day, never wanting to come down.

"I think about that day a lot." He smiled wryly. "It was, like, the best day of my life."

We both sat silent a moment, reflecting.

"I'm sorry I didn't call," he murmured.

"Not a big deal," I said, rising to my feet, though the world kind of twirled around me. "I need to get to class."

I hobbled away, holding the can to my head—an Ice Queen.

Conner had me mega confused. What did he want? He didn't seem to know. So how could I possibly figure it out? It left me feeling vulnerable. One minute he was looking at me with longing in his eyes, talking about the past, the next he was kissing Laura.

I tried to get him out of my head. Tried getting *everything* out of my head.

My head hurt.

It had an ugly black and blue bump on it.

And when I got home from work, I was tired. Beat. That's probably why I didn't notice Brian Abbott's Honda parked across the street when I pulled into the driveway.

"Hi!" he said as soon as I opened my car door.

"Ahhhggg!" I jumped about a mile in the air.

I'd been forcing practices on him like a mad woman. So now, I tried not to hold it against him that he almost gave me a heart attack. After all, I owed him big time.

"Brian, what—what are you doing here?" I tried to smile and act friendly, as though it was perfectly normal to see him at my house in the middle of the night. But it wasn't, and it kind of freaked me out, a little.

"Raven and I—we had a big fight," Brian said. "She just doesn't understand me." Brian gave my arm a squeeze. "Not the way you do."

Huh?

I took a step away from him, realizing I'd brought this on myself. I had been heaping compliments on him like crazy, telling him how smart he was, what a great singer he was. And I'd been listening to all of his long, drawn out stories as though he was the most fascinating person on earth.

But I'd felt like I had to, like I owed it to him. I mean, I made him practice *all* the time, all semester long. I'd made him practice, practice, practice. But now that the competition was actually approaching, I may have gone a little overboard, even for me.

Okay, so I began worrying about that once Raven started in with her dirty looks. And, yeah, I noticed Brian starting to act a little strange around me, too; sort of flirty-like. It was weird. So yes, I did *sort of* start to worry that I was giving him the wrong impression. That maybe all my desperate demands for practices seemed a little excessive. Like maybe they left him thinking I was trying to find excuses to get close to him.

I would have backed off. I would have. Only I really, really wanted to win. I *needed* it. Like I said, I think it had something subconscious to do with losing Conner. But I didn't take the time to analyze it. All I knew was, I had to win.

I'd thought about having a heart-to-heart with Brian. But I kind of kept telling myself I didn't need to. That I was imagining things. After all, we were in honor choir together. And I *did* always stress that I wanted to win, and he had a girlfriend. He had to know I wasn't coming on to him, right?

Wrong, I guess.

The next words out of his mouth were, "I can't stop thinking about you."

I blinked.

Brian used to visually cringe whenever he saw me coming, because he knew what I always wanted—to practice. Hence, the cookies and compliments and listening and stuff. Obviously, these were more powerful tools than I'd realized.

I stared at Brian.

It was late. I was tired. And I knew what I had to do. "Brian," I said, "did you know I'm a Mormon?"

"Uh, yeah. I'd heard something about that," he said, sounding confused, as though wondering why I was bringing it up. So, I enlightened him.

"Well, I don't drink or go to parties. And the boys I date can't drink or go to parties and they have to be Mormon." I looked at him inquisitively. "Do you want me to send the missionaries over to your house?"

Brian took a step back. "Uh, well, no. I don't think so."

"No?" I tried to sound disappointed. After all, I still needed him to be my partner. "Well, that's okay, I guess. I understand. You and Raven make a really cute couple."

Brian looked confused. "Thanks."

My work here finished, I started for the house, but then turned back. "Why don't you invite Raven to our next practice?" I said, feeling inspired. "How about tomorrow morning before school?"

chapter 15

Raven came to our next duet practice, but she *still* gave me dirty looks. I tried to put myself in her shoes, though. After all, I remembered how unhappy I was when Conner and I were still together and he started spending so much time with Laura. Let me tell you, I was one scowling puppy.

But still, I was bummed. Discouraged. I'd thought inviting Raven to come to our practices would help, but it didn't. She and Brian argued the whole time. About everything. It was like watching a bad made-for-TV movie—a lame one that you'd change the channel on, only the remote is clear across the room and you're mega tired. But it seemed too contrived. No one in true life could fight *that* much.

Only, apparently, they could.

Because they did.

And it was bringing me down. Big time.

"Don't you think we're way better than the last time you saw us?" I asked Raven, trying to get rid of the thick, dark cloud hovering in the room. Trying to bring in a little light.

She rolled her eyes. "Yeah. I guess."

I smiled broadly, acting as though she had exclaimed, "Oh yes! You're great!"

"Me too!" I said enthusiastically.

Raven just rolled her eyes again.

When the bell finally rang for class, I practically did cartwheels I was so excited to get away. *Free! Free! At last free!*

"See ya," I said, and ran for the door.

64

*   *   *   *   *

Trent raised his eyebrows when he saw me at lunch. "What happened to you?"

I put my hand over the huge, black bruise on my forehead. "Conner did it."

I was explaining yesterday's episode when Caitlin passed by. Of course, she stopped to shoot the breeze, being as cheerful as always.

"I know this isn't really happening, Trent," she said. "You suddenly changing so much. Suddenly going to school dances and dating 'Megan the Mormon.'" She was about to march away, but then turned back, saying it again, "Megan the Mormon!" She huffed it as though it was inconceivable. "What are you going to do, Trent?" she sneered. "Stop drinking and start going to church?"

Trent took my hand, looking into my eyes. Suddenly, I couldn't move. Or breathe. Or remember my name. "Maybe," he said.

Caitlin, Nina, and I—we all blinked. "Huh?"

Caitlin shook her head with disgust. "This is too much."

This time she did storm away, fuming.

I took a sip of my water, trying to gain composure. But I could still feel the warmth of Trent's hand. *It's just an act*, I told myself. The hand holding, the words, all of it—just an act. But it was hard to convince myself of that. Because it didn't feel like an act, not to me.

chapter 16

Saturday morning, the day of the dance, I found myself sitting in front of the phone, unsure what to do. Today was a primary activity, and for a personal progress goal, I was helping out.

As I was getting ready, I got this great idea to invite Wendy to come along, but I wasn't sure whom to call. Wendy, herself? I wasn't sure if that was a good idea. I didn't want her mom to get the wrong idea and think I was trying to pressure Wendy into coming to our church.

After giving it a lot of thought, I figured I should probably talk to Mrs. Ryan herself. Only the lady didn't know me and I didn't know her and the phone conversation might be kind of awkward and I'm not always so good on the phone with people I don't know.

So, of course I knew the best thing to do would be to talk to Trent about it and let him handle his family. Only, I wasn't quite sure I was up to calling Trent. Sure, we'd been getting closer, becoming friends, but I didn't want to give him the impression I was forgetting all of this was only an act, just part of our deal. I didn't want to make him worry I was starting to fall for it. That I was going to, you know, stalk him.

"It's for Wendy," I told myself. "Get over your geek-o-rama and do it for her."

I knew she would enjoy the activity. So, I took a deep breath and dialed the Ryan's number. But it was Trent who answered the phone, and hearing his voice got me all spazzy.

My palms were suddenly soaked. I quickly wiped them on my jeans, saying, "Hello. May I speak to Mrs. Ryan, please?" For some

66

reason, I tried sounding like a business-person.

"Is this Megan?"

I wanted to smack my head with the phone. "Uh, yeah. Hi, Trent."

"Hi." He sounded surprised that I'd called. "My mom is Mrs. Hayes," he said. "My dad died. She remarried."

"Oh." Wendy had told me that before, but I'd completely forgotten.

"Do you want me to get my mom?" Trent asked.

"Uh, no. I was just wondering if Wendy might like to come to a kid's activity at our church this afternoon. They're making gifts for mother's day. I'm helping at it, so I'll be there to help her and everything."

"Yeah," Trent said. "She would probably like that. Only, if you're going to be working, maybe I should go with her, to help her."

"You can, that would be great. But you don't have to. She'll be fine."

"Well," Trent didn't sound convinced. "I'll just go. Just to make sure."

* * * * *

By the time Trent and Wendy showed up at the church, I was already covered in flour. The kids were measuring out the dry ingredients for chocolate-chip cookies and filling them layer by layer into canning jars. But, they were kids, so it was a messy job—besides the fact I'd gotten into a couple of flour fights.

"This is how you get ready for a big 'cool' dance?" Trent asked with a grin, saying the word "cool" as though it was anything but. "Covering yourself in flour?"

I flicked a dab of it at him. Then made a pose. "What? You don't like this look?"

He raised his eyebrows. "I do. It's great." The way he said it—so completely sincere—gave me the desperate need to look away, appear busy. I quickly scooped a cup of flour into Josh Taylor's canning jar, realizing too late, I'd already given him a scoop.

I made a harried mental note to catch the kid later, give him a jar with the correct ingredients. But I couldn't do it now. Trent was staring at me and I was internally spazzing out.

He asked, "Aren't you supposed to be doing your nails or getting your hair done or something?"

I got the impression he was impressed that I wasn't doing those things. So, I didn't mention that I planned to do them the minute I got home. Instead, I acted offended, placing my hands on my hips. "You don't like my hair? But I spent hours getting it to do this!"

I'd quickly harnessed it back into a pony this morning, not even bothering to wash it since I planned to put it through the works later, and now it was full of flour. I'm sure it looked delightful.

Sister Springsteed wiggled her finger at us, playfully. "More work, less chatter," she said.

I scooped up a cupful of flour, pouring it into another canning jar, this time making sure I hadn't already done it. At the same moment, Sara Woodland from Wendy's primary class offered to take Wendy around to the activities. Besides the cookie jars, they were also making their mothers paper roses and necklaces made from colored cereal rings.

Wendy looked up at Trent eagerly. "Can I go with her?"

Trent was hesitant.

"She'll be fine," Sara coaxed. "I'll help her."

"Okay," Trent said cautiously. "Wendy, I'll be right here if you need me."

Trent watched his little sister run off with Sara. I could tell he was happy for her, but a little worried too.

"Sara's a good kid," I said.

"Yeah, she seems like it," Trent agreed. "But sometimes kids are pretty brutal. Even the ones that seem nice."

Trent smiled at me, brushing away his dark thoughts. "I guess I can help you out here. I'll just check on her now and then, without her seeing. She thinks I'm overprotective."

I smiled at that, saying nothing.

He grinned. "What? You agree?"

"No. It's nice." I laughed, thinking of him sitting in primary for the last two weeks with all the little ten-year-olds. Most likely, the girls all fell madly in love with him, while the boys all wanted to be just like him. With Trent around, Wendy was probably the most popular kid in class.

Trent grabbed a measuring cup and helped the kids scoop out ingredients with me.

"So, you're volunteering *again*," he said with a grin. "Anywhere help is needed, you're there. Like a super hero." He made a trumpeting noise. "Look, it's Volunteer Woman."

Just then he opened a bag of flour a little too aggressively. Flour flew everywhere.

I laughed. "Hey, you got my cape dirty." I flung some flour back in his direction. And that was the beginning of a flour fight.

"Truce," Trent called, dusted with flour, laughing as I was about to stuff a handful down his shirt.

By now, we were both covered from head to toe. So, I acted concerned, "Do I have flour on my face?"

He scrutinized me. "Wait. We missed a spot." He smeared more flour across my cheek. "There. Perfect."

"Thanks!"

He asked for it! I stuffed my handful down his shirt.

Then, of course, we quickly cleaned up our mess—super quick, like lightening. Before Sister Springsteed could see, and scold us again. She runs a tight kitchen.

Believe it or not, even the clean up was a blast. Everything was fun with Trent. Everything!

When the activity was over, Trent smiled, seeming pleased. "Wendy had a good time," he said. "We both did." He seemed hesitant to leave, but he backed away anyway, as there wasn't anything left to do. "Well, see you."

He headed for the door, but then turned back to me as though just remembering, "Hey, tonight. I'll see you tonight."

I raised my eyebrows. He better not forget!

"Right," was all I said, but under my breath added, "In five hours and twenty-seven minutes."

Obviously, my mind was a little more on the dance than his.

chapter 17

We were double dating with Nina and Justin for the dance. Dad wouldn't let me go alone with a non-member boy. It was just as well. I hoped I would be less of a spaz with Nina by my side. I knew I could count on her to give me a kick if I started to dork out.

I spent like an hour on my hair, trying to force it into this fancy 'do I'd spotted in a magazine. It had step-by-step instructions and everything. But I'm not hair competent, and it didn't work, and finally, I gave up, re-washed it, and wore it down, full and normal.

I zipped up my dress just as the doorbell rang. So I only had a moment to admire my image in the mirror, but I actually did admire it. For once. A seamstress had specially tailored the dress, so it actually fit nicely. The way it was supposed to. I was amazed. I didn't look twelve.

The way Trent gazed at me as I came down the stairs made me feel confident I looked okay.

"Wow." He raised his eyebrows. "You look—wow."

Suddenly, I felt shy. I was torn between wanting to race back upstairs, and wanting to jump into his arms. Yowza, yowza! He looked hot.

"Just breathe," I told myself. How do you do that again?

Trent gave me a beautiful wrist corsage, and a wrapped package. I stared at the gift with bewilderment, then gazed up at him. "What's this?"

"Just a . . ." He brushed away his attempt to answer. "Just open it."

I looked up at Mom and Dad. They shrugged, looking pleased,

but just as bewildered as I was. I opened the box, then dropped my jaw. It was the elegant wrap from Jordan's!

"I thought you'd like it for tonight," Trent said. "Since you looked so *stunning* in it and everything."

My face reddened as my parent's didn't have a clue Trent was teasing me. They probably thought he was in love with me or something. I would have explained the whole thing to them—only I was stunned speechless by his gift. Why would Trent do this? Why would he buy me such an extraordinary gift? Why would he buy me a gift at all?

"I . . ." I didn't know what to say. My parents were standing right there. I knew they wouldn't let me take such an expensive gift from a boy. "Thank you so much, Trent. Really. But I don't think I can accept it."

"No. Accept it," Trent said, refusing to take the box back as I tried to give it to him. "Your song—I played it and I didn't even ask you if I could."

"Well, you can," I told him quickly. "I was flattered that you wanted to."

"So, take the gift," he said. "Your song's amazing. You deserve it." I looked at my parents.

"It's beautiful," Mom said, placing the wrap over my shoulders.

I guessed that meant it was okay. I was glad, because I loved it. I didn't want to have to give it back. I'd treasure it forever and ever. Especially because Trent gave it to me. He actually went back to Jordan's and bought it. That touched me so much I could have cried. Right then and there. Even as Mom and Dad snapped picture after picture of us, posing us this way and that.

When we got to Nina's, her parents were snapping off a roll of film of her and Justin. They were digitizing movies too. No wonder. Justin was every parent's dream catch for their daughter. (He was an Eagle Scout and everything.)

The only problem was, Nina had to ask *him* to the dance. His long-time girlfriend, Nicole, had just dumped him. For weeks now he'd been moping around, looking lost and sad.

The only one out of the four of us who wasn't on the rebound was Nina. Boy, weren't we in for a fun night?

*   *   *   *   *

The night was turning out perfect. We'd had a wonderful dinner at a romantic Italian Bistro, and I had begun to settle down a little, feeling comfortable on Trent's arm, until we entered the dance. Then it was a new experience all over again.

It was kind of fun having everyone stare at us. And stare, they did. They were probably wondering what was so special about me. Wondering why Trent had broken his rule and brought me, Megan The Mormon, of all people, to the dance. It was a fair question. But I didn't have the answer. I was as clueless as anyone else. I was simply glad he brought me.

To be honest, the stares were all right. I was prepared for them. But I also noticed a bunch of dirty looks from various people (namely Caitlin, Aspen, Laura, and Conner). However, I was pretty much able to overlook them, since I was having the most incredible night of my life. Trent was an awesome escort, even if it didn't seem as though we were going to actually dance.

Instead we talked with friends, and sometimes just each other. And it was great. Perfect. I loved being with Trent. Loved that he was my date. That he had brought me here and bought me dinner, and my beautiful wrap. I was in heaven. What did I care if we danced or not?

Still, I couldn't help wondering what it would be like to have Trent take me in his arms, and ...

Stop it! I scolded myself on more than one occasion. Trent doesn't dance. Don't torture yourself dreaming about it. Just enjoy being here with him. He's being so nice and sweet and considerate. Enjoy it while you can. After tonight the deal is over. Face it, he may never talk to you again.

I did, of course, listen to myself, as I was wise and full of great wisdom. I loved being with Trent, and getting his devoted, undivided attention was something special that I would cherish forever and ever. It was wonderful. Everything was wonderful.

So, I enjoyed it. Majorly.

Only, at one point, I found myself staring at Conner and Laura out on the dance floor. I couldn't help thinking about past dances when it had been me in Conner's arms, me he whispered to as we swayed to the music.

"Do you want to dance?" The words were whispered in my ear, sending my heart aflutter.

Huh?

I whipped around to face Trent.

"Wh—what?" I stammered, embarrassed that he'd caught me watching Conner and Laura. I'd probably had a wistful, woebegone look on my face. And now he felt sorry for me.

I reddened. "No. That's okay. I know you don't like to dance."

"What are you talking about?" Trent said, leading me onto the dance floor. "I *love* to dance."

I laughed at the way he said that, especially because I knew it was so untrue, but my laughter stopped when he took me into his arms. Then my heart sped up, and my mouth went dry.

"We're good together," he said.

It was so true I couldn't even speak.

All I could do was think, "This is the best night of my life."

*   *   *   *   *

After that slow dance, Trent and I danced every dance for a long, long while. I was having a blast. And to my bliss and utter surprise, Trent was too. He seemed as surprised as anyone. But boy oh boy, could that boy dance!

I was starting to work up a sweat.

"I'll be right back," I told Trent, heading for the girls' room. On my way, with my luck, I stepped in a wad of gum.

"Great!" I muttered.

I tried scraping it off in the bathroom. I grated it for like, ever against the rim of the smelly trash can. But no use. It was still sort of sticky. It would bug me when I danced.

Grrrr!

I looked around in frustration. I didn't want to spend the rest of the-best-night-of-my-life trying to get gum off my shoe! Finally, I found a nail file (on the yucky bathroom floor!) and used that. I had to sit in a stall while I scraped. Stunning.

When I got back to the gym, I looked all over for Trent. Finally, I spotted him across the room. Caitlin had him cornered. Poor Trent! He was all alone, while Caitlin had her arm draped around Shane Franks. I knew what he must be going through. I felt it every time I saw Conner and Laura together. He needed me. I rushed to Trent's rescue, flinging my arms around him as though I did that sort of thing all of the time.

"There you are," I said, maybe a little over-loudly because I was nervous about what I was going to do. I kissed him. On the mouth. And it turned out kind of passionate-like, though I hadn't meant it to.

"This is *not* happening," Caitlin growled, leading Shane toward the door.

When I pulled away, Trent looked bewildered and amazed. "I thought you said no kissing."

"I meant you can't kiss me," I told him, breathlessly. "I can kiss you."

He raised his eyebrows, still looking amazed. "Obviously."

I felt wobbly, like I might topple over, and it had nothing to do with my high-heels.

"Let's dance," I said, acting as though that was why I was suddenly leaning against him. But really, it was that kiss. It had me weak in the knees. Woozy. I honestly had only meant it to be a sweet, little peck, not fireworks. What happened?

But just dancing with Trent did strange, unexpected things to me, left me feeling giddy. I closed my eyes and pretended he was really my boyfriend, that this wasn't all a strange act. And maybe some of it wasn't . . . right? I mean, he didn't have to buy me the wrap.

What did he *do* that for?

In the bathroom, when I told Nina about the gift, she jumped up and down saying how romantic it was. "He loves you," she gasped. "He *adores* you."

I bit my lip. I knew that wasn't true. It couldn't be. "Maybe it's just like he said," I told her. "Maybe he just bought it to thank me for letting him use my song. And he's incredibly nice. He saw me drooling over it in the store. He probably just decided to take pity on a sad, pathetic soul."

"He's incredibly nice?" Nina raised her eyebrows, starting to jump all over again. "You love him. You *adore* him."

"I do," I admitted distraughtly. "I love him. I adore him."

As I said, that whole conversation took place in the girls' bathroom. That is, after I checked under all the stall doors to make sure Nina and I were alone. I would never, ever admit my pathetic predicament to anyone else in the whole world. It was more than just a crush. I was in deep, head-over-heels like with Trent Ryan, the coolest guy in school. Tragedy, tragedy, tragedy!

chapter 18

"Why did you even bother to take me to the dance?"

Like everyone else, I whipped around to see who was yelling. I widened my eyes when I saw who it was—Laura! She was yelling at Conner out on the dance floor.

Conner tried to calm her down, stop her from making a bigger scene. But Laura pulled away from him saying no, she wouldn't calm down. I got the feeling she had been drinking, a lot. She seemed unsteady as she yelled, "You've been staring at her all night. Why didn't you just take *her* to the dance?"

Laura stormed away, and Conner followed after her. I watched them go feeling a mixture of things: curiosity, bewilderment, shock. But something else too. I couldn't help it—I felt sorry for Conner. He hates scenes almost as much as I do.

Nina rushed over to me, dragging Justin with her. "You know that was about you, right?" Her eyes were round with excitement. "I told you he's been looking at you all night."

Nina *had* mentioned, about a hundred times, that Conner was staring at me. Looking at me longingly. Looking at me as though he was sad that it was Trent holding me in his arms rather than him. But the thing about Nina is, she's a romantic. The hopeless kind. She reads romance into everything. So, as much as I'd wanted to believe her that Conner was dejected and pining for me, I just didn't.

But now, I guess I had to take what she was saying as at least plausible because Trent agreed. "Yeah," he said. "The guy's been staring at you all night."

I tilted my head. "He has?"

I guess I'd gotten too wrapped up in being in Trent's arms to pay much attention to Conner. That realization made me smile.

Only, I think Trent took the smile to be happiness that Conner was finally missing me. 'Cause his next words were, "So, I guess our deal worked. Caitlin's bugged, Conner's remorseful." He shrugged. "Good job, huh?"

I had a funny feeling in my stomach. Like this was the end of our deal. Like Trent felt it was complete. But I didn't want it to be. It wasn't over! Not yet. I . . . didn't want it to be.

"Can we dance some more?" I said, trying to keep the desperation out of my voice.

He looked at me quizzically. "Sure."

It was a slow dance, and he took me in his arms and I held on to him super tight. I didn't want to let go, not ever. All night, he had been so, so incredibly sweet. It was like a fairy tale—but I didn't want it to be a fairy tale. At the stroke of midnight I didn't want to have to leave the Ball. I wanted the Ball to go on forever.

Suddenly, I was tapped on the shoulder. I turned with surprise. It was Conner. "Can I cut in for a second?"

I looked up at Trent questioningly. "Sure," he said, backing away. "I'll be outside."

Conner took me in his arms, and it felt different than being with Trent. Not better, but extremely comfortable, like old times.

"I thought you left," I told him.

"I did. I took Laura home. But I couldn't get you out of my head."

It was only now that I realized something. I could smell *alcohol* on him. Conner had been drinking!

Just this Sunday he had stood up on the stand saying how important and special the church was to him, and yet what did he turn around and do tonight? He drank! Realizing that was enough to make me cry. But Conner went on, breaking my heart. "I can't take this," he said. "I miss you. I miss us. Laura and I, we're over. I mean it. It was a mistake, the whole thing. I see that now."

It was strange to hear him say this, the exact words I wanted to hear, had desperately longed to hear. But I hadn't pictured it like this, his spouting it with alcohol on his breath.

Still, even with that, I could have forgiven him. Chucked it up to being under a bad influence. Bad, bad Laura. That seemed to be what he was expecting, telling me how he needed my "guidance" in his life.

No joke, I could have so easily forgiven him, let things go back to the way they were. I was tempted to. Pathetic, but true. Only I kept remembering a conversation we'd had right after our break-up:

"You made everything so complicated," Conner had said. "I got further with Laura on our first date than I ever did with you, ever."

He'd said that to me. It had made me feel like he was a stranger. Someone I didn't know. Someone I didn't *want* to know.

And this whole time we were apart—his avoiding the church, and drinking, and no longer being able to take the sacrament . . .

No, things couldn't go back to the way they were. They couldn't. Not ever. He had changed—or, rather, he was never what I'd thought. And he had betrayed me. Betrayed my trust. And now he had done things I didn't even want to know about. Things that made him unworthy to take the sacrament. He wasn't my Cody any more. Now he was just Conner, a guy I used to date.

Conner's next words made me blink. "So can I give you a ride home? And we'll start over?"

I gazed at him as though he'd lost his brain, because really it seemed he had. "No," I told him. "You can't take me home. Trent brought me here. Trent will take me home."

"Megan, you don't know that guy. He's just playing games with you. He's a player. That's what he does. He gets a girl to fall for him, breaks her heart, then he's on to another girl." Conner ran his hands through his hair. "It's a game."

I bit my lip. Maybe that was true. I'd seen it happen a lot, girls falling for Trent. Him roaming from girl to girl. But Trent seemed so sincere. Was that part of his act?

"Look," I said, trying to sound more confident than I actually felt, "this has nothing to do with anything but the dance. I came with Trent and I'm leaving with Trent."

"Megan, I can't take it, seeing you with that guy!"

I just tilted my head. It hadn't exactly been a party seeing him with Laura. What did he think I'd been doing? Dancing a jig? "Go home Conner," I told him. But when he started to walk away, I thought better of it. Suddenly, I was concerned.

I grabbed his arm. "How much did you drink?"

He furrowed his brow. "Drink?"

He seemed embarrassed that I knew. He tried to deny it. But finally he said, "Geez, Megan, I'm not drunk. Don't worry about it."

But I *was* worried. I didn't hang around people who drank. I had no idea how much was too much. All I knew was, you're not supposed to drink and drive.

"We'll give you a ride," I told him.

He widened his eyes incredulously. "You and your new boyfriend?"

"Just to be safe."

He looked at me as though I was nuts. "I'm not getting in a car with that guy. Talk about drunk, the guy drinks like a fish. He's the one you should be worried about."

"He didn't drink tonight," I said.

Conner scoffed at the idea, both that Trent hadn't drank, and that we would give him a ride home. "I'm not getting in a car with that guy," Conner said adamantly. "If you're that worried about me, you can give me a ride. But not him."

I put my hands on my hips. "Fine," I relented at last.

He really didn't seem drunk. He was probably fine to drive home. After all, he had driven Laura there and gotten back in one piece. But I couldn't take that chance. If he were to get into an accident.. . .

I had to go outside and explain the situation to Trent. I felt awful. But he took it well. Actually, he didn't seem to care one way or the other. Which kind of hurt. A lot.

"Well, it was fun," he said. "Dancing and everything."

I smiled. "Yeah."

We stood a moment, looking at each other.

"Well, drive carefully," he said.

"Yeah. Uh, okay," I stammered, backing away. "Thanks."

I guess to him, the deal was over. A big success. That sort of made me want to cry.

chapter 19

I tromped into Conner's car feeling resentful. He had ruined the last of my evening with Trent. And it was my last evening!

I drove him home in silence, stewing.

It was weird to be feeling this way, full of resentment. After all, here I was, alone with Conner. It wasn't long ago I'd have given my left arm for a chance like this, being alone with him, having him tell me how much he's missed me. But the thing was, if I hadn't gone to the dance with Trent, if I had stayed home, lonely and miserable, would this moment even be happening? I doubted it. If I had stayed lonely and miserable Conner would have been perfectly happy to trot off with Laura. He just couldn't stand to see me, his loyal puppy dog, actually moving on. Getting a life. Falling in love.

I pulled up in front of Conner's house.

"Do you want to come in?" he asked. "We could make banana splits, like we used to after a dance." He grinned. "And then drink hot chocolate to warm us up."

It seemed he was taking it for granted I had forgiven him. That since I left the dance with him, obviously all was well. That bugged me. But maybe he was right. Maybe the old me would have been like that. Just caved in. After all, I used to think Conner was the greatest. He could do no wrong. But well, he had proven that theory full of holes. Pretty continuously, lately.

Still, making banana splits after dances had been fun. And dating Conner had been fun. Nice. Most of the time.

Sad to say, the coming-in-and-reliving-old-times bit was actually kinda tempting. Super tempting, actually.

"No," I sighed. "I'm tired. I want to go home."

Conner sounded resigned. "Okay," he said, getting out of his car. "But will you at least think about what I've said?"

What did he say? That he's sorry? That he realized he had made a terrible mistake? Those were all things I had dreamed of hearing from him. *Of course* I would think about them. They just wouldn't mean as much to me as they once would have.

"Yes," I said. "I'll think about it."

I watched Conner walk away, still unsure how I felt. Did I want him back? Really and truly? A huge part of me (Stupid! Stupid! Stupid!) was still dying to answer, "Yes." But another part of me, a calmer, wiser, saner part of me, was saying, "No." Our time was over. It had been special, but not nearly as special as I had once thought. His actions had proven that. And it was over.

Definitely over . . . I hoped.

I just had to be strong.

But watching Conner, my very first boyfriend, walk away, romantically out of my life forever, left me in tears. And that's the way I drove home, bawling my eyes out. I parked Conner's car out in front of my house, then ran upstairs to my room.

I flung myself across my bed, and my parents were at my door in record speed, wanting to know what happened. What had that non-member boy done to me? Why was I so upset?

I, of course, didn't want to talk to them. I wanted to bawl in privacy. But I couldn't have them thinking Trent had hurt me, not even for a second.

"It wasn't Trent," I sobbed. "It was Conner. We broke up."

My parents looked at each other quizzically. After all, Conner and I had broken up over two months ago. But to me, this night, it was like we had broken up all over again. Only tonight it was different because I had chose to do it. Which, of course, was better. Way better. But it was still traumatizing, because I couldn't help it, I still loved him. Maybe not as much, or the same, but as stupid as it was, I still had deep feelings for him.

"You mean you had a fight?" Mom asked.

I shook my head, still sobbing. "No. Not really." I smooshed my face into my pillow. "I don't want to talk about it."

Mom patted my back sympathetically. Then she gave me a soft kiss on the back of my head. "We understand," she said.

Then they left. Mom and Dad left! Abandoned me, in my hour of need.

I cried for an hour. But then, I kind of stopped thinking about Conner. About our past dances. About our past life. And I started to think about *this* dance. About Trent. About how much fun we'd had. And how sweet he was. And how I'd been gypped out of my good night kiss.

I had an overwhelming urge to talk to him. Tonight. As wonderful as the dance had been, I hated the way it ended. Just thinking about it left my stomach in knots. Darn Conner! I wanted to *talk* to Trent. Explain better why I had to drive Conner home. Thank him for taking me to the dance. And for being so wonderful and thoughtful and kind, and absolutely everything I wanted in a boy. Except . . . he wasn't Mormon.

I rolled over in my bed. I would never sleep. Not tonight.

Trent was *like* a Mormon. He was good and kind. And honest. He seemed very honest. And, sure, he used to drink, but that was only because he didn't know any better. He didn't use to know about the Church. But now he did, a little. And he'd come to church two Sundays in a row. That had to count for something. And he didn't drink at the dance. Or any other time that I knew of in the last two weeks.

And maybe he would come to church again tomorrow. Well, not, tomorrow. Tomorrow was conference, but maybe he would come to church again, sometime. And who knows, maybe he would become a Mormon!

The thought made me smile. But then, reality had to come pushing its nosy way in. Face it, I thought, it would be a miracle if Trent Ryan, Mr. Party Guy, became a Mormon.

But it wasn't really *that* impossible, not to me. Not anymore. I could definitely picture it. After all, he had come to church twice in a row, and he had gone a whole Saturday night without drinking. Maybe Mr. Party Animal was changing.

I rolled over in bed again. *No! Stop it!* I told myself. Don't torture yourself like this. But I couldn't help it. To me, it was possible. To me, Trent really did seem interested in the church . . . and me. Okay, I didn't have any concrete evidence. No evidence at all, really. It was just a feeling I got. But it was a strong feeling, sort of.

I got out of bed, and went over to my computer. Sometimes, Trent and I chatted on line. Not very often. Well, actually, just once. But we could do it again. Now. You never know, he *could* be on line. Not that I held out much hope. After all, it was very, very late, and hours past the dance. Most likely he was in bed, sound asleep. Still, I thought I'd give it a try. As I said, you never know. And I really, really wanted to talk to him. Really.

And guess what?

He was on line!

I instant messaged him on iChat: "Hi."

He iChatted me back: "Did you have fun at the dance?"

"Yes!" I wrote. "That's what I wanted to tell you. I had a blast. Thank you so much for taking me!"

"Are you in love with me?"

I rubbed my eyes, staring at the question. Why'd he ask *that*?

"Do you think I love you?" was next. Then, "That I'll turn Mormon?"

Huh?

I stared at the screen, my stomach suddenly a ball of knots. What was going on? Why was he writing this? I was afraid to press a key. Afraid to answer. What was I supposed to say?

Nothing showed up for a long time. Then:

"Forget it. Look, Megan, Trent's not here at the moment. So don't freak out. It's me, Caitlin."

Caitlin?

A knife was plunged into my heart. I was bleeding all over the floor. Caitlin? *Caitlin?* Why was she there? At his house? I felt sick realizing they must have gotten back together.

A knife was in my heart. My eyes stung. My stomach ached. I was practically doubled over with pain. Yet Caitlin went on, writing as though we were best friends having a nice ichat. "Trent went down to his basement to get us a drink," she wrote. "Should I tell him you messaged or called, or whatever?"

"No."

I clicked off my computer and crawled back into bed, wrenching out huge, painful sobs into my pillow. My life was a tragic, cruel joke.

chapter 20

I woke late on Sunday. Since it was general conference, I laid around all morning in my pajamas, moping. Thinking about last night. The good stuff and the bad stuff. There had been a lot of both. I thought a lot about what Conner had said. About me being a "guidance" in his life. But, you know, I wasn't sure I wanted to "guide" someone through life. I mean, what about me? I could use some guidance too. I saw the women in our ward with non-active or non-member husbands. They had to carry the whole load—bringing their kids to church, sitting alone. It seemed hard and lonely. It wasn't what I wanted.

And thinking about Trent was just as difficult. More difficult. I'd had a wonderful time at the dance. He had been so sweet and thoughtful, and he'd given me my beautiful wrap. But after the dance. I hated to think about that, but I had to. I had to look at reality. Caitlin was at his house. Most likely they had gotten back together. (Sigh.) And he'd gone to his basement to get them a "drink." Caitlin had made a point of saying that. I kind of figured she didn't mean root beers.

Unfortunately, even if Caitlin and Trent didn't get back together, even if she was at his house just because, I don't know, she and Shane got into a fight and she needed a shoulder to cry on. Whatever innocent reason. (And there were gobs to choose from . . . right?) Still, I had to face the cold, hard truth, once and for all: Trent wasn't a guy I could date. He just wasn't, because as cute and nice and sweet as he was, still, he wasn't right for me. As my Laurel advisor, Sister Green, was always saying, "Be discerning who you date. He may just be your future mate." Something like that.

And I didn't want someone who drank for a future husband. I didn't want that sort of life. I wanted a husband who could hold the priesthood, take me to the temple, and help me raise our children in the Church. I wanted an eternal family. A forever family. And Trent couldn't give me that.

"As if he even wanted to," I grumbled. As if he even wanted to *date* me!

After all, the minute the dance was over he was back with Caitlin. And got them "drinks."

And, besides, I made everything too complicated. Conner had told me that. Caitlin, I'm sure, made everything easy. And wasn't that what all high school boys wanted? The easy girl?

So, needless to say, my Sunday was kind of dark, and when Conner came to pick up his car, he didn't exactly brighten it. He had on sunglasses and complained of a headache. Signs of a hang over, right?

"I want to talk to you later, okay?" he said, pressing his hands against his forehead. "But right now, I'm feeling kind of sick."

I nodded. "Okay."

I was in no hurry to have "the talk." I didn't really even know what to tell him. Well, that wasn't exactly true. I knew what I *should* tell him. I just didn't know if I would be able to actually get the words out.

But the honest truth was, I knew we shouldn't get back together. I knew it even before we broke up—we shouldn't be together any more. Because he was lying to me and how can you date a person you can't even trust? But I'd clung to him anyway, because it is one thing to know what is right, and a total other thing to actually do it. And the knowing is way easier than the doing.

But it was more than just the horrible things Conner had done at the last of our dating, things he tried chalking up to "sparing my feelings." It was all those things he'd done since our break up.

Sure, Conner had said he learned a lesson from the mistakes he made with Laura. And I'm glad he learned. But the more I thought about it, the more I realized Trent was right. Conner wasn't good enough for me.

*   *   *   *   *

Monday morning, Nina rushed up to me in a panic as I fought with my locker. Sometimes, I swear, the thing changes its combination over night.

"Did you hear about Brian?!" Nina gasped.

I kicked my locker. "Brian Abbott?"

Nina huffed impatiently. "Of course Brian Abbott! What other Brian is there?"

Since the competition against Roosevelt High was right around the corner, Brian Abbott was dang important in my life. But lets face it, there were a lot of other Brians in the world. Right here at our school, in fact. For instance, there was Brian Sharp in my pre-calculus class. And there was that cute junior, Brian Foster. But when I tried to share this information with Nina, she sort of exploded.

"Brian Abbott!" she snapped. "I'm talking about Brian Abbott. Over the weekend he got into a huge fight with Raven, and then his mom, and now he moved to Colorado to live with his dad."

I grabbed her shoulders. "No!" Then I shook her. "You're kidding, right? Tell me you're kidding."

Nina removed my hands from her shoulders. Then she backed a safe distance away before saying, "I'm not kidding. He's gone."

"But I need him!"

I couldn't let Hailey win again this semester. I just couldn't. I had groomed Brian all year, perfected him. Lately, at practice I could almost smell our victory. That's how close we were. But now it seemed to be slipping away.

"No, no, no!" I cried, as though denying it would change things. But it didn't. After my tantrum, Brian was still gone.

I slunk through my morning classes, dejected. During Madrigals, Mr. Smith seemed as destitute as me when he learned Brian had ditched us. "Well, Megan," Mr. Smith scratched his whiskery chin in contemplation, "there's always Phil."

I bowed my head, wanting to bow out of the competition. My dream was over. Done. Finished. But just then I saw Trent saunter by our class.

It gave me an idea, a really great one!

"What if I know someone with an amazing voice? He isn't in Madrigals, or the choir, but he goes to our school. Could he take Brian's place?"

Mr. Smith's eyes brightened. "Sure. Can you get him to sing with you?"

My heart sank a little. Sank a lot. No. I probably couldn't get Trent to sing with me. He was considered cool and being in Madrigals wasn't. Not by a long shot. Not to his crowd, anyway. He probably wouldn't be caught dead singing with us.

"I don't know," I told Mr. Smith anyway, giving the poor man false hope. "I'll ask him."

How could I get Trent to sing the duet with me?

Suddenly I was on a quest.

chapter 21

I didn't see Trent for the rest of the day. He didn't come sit with me at lunch, just as I knew he wouldn't. Our deal was over. Finished. Instead he was off with his cool friends, doing cool things. I missed him.

In the cafeteria, as I was wolfing down my burrito (I love the school's burritos. They *fry* them.) Conner approached, sitting across from Nina and me. Shock!

I covered my mouth with a napkin, embarrassed that my mouth was so full, because it was F-U-L-L. Back when Trent used to eat with us, I was always Miss Dainty-eater, careful to take teeny, little bites, in case I thought of something clever to say. (As if!) Of course, being with Trent had been enough to sustain me. I didn't really need to eat at all. But now he was gone. And I was hungry.

"Did you think about what I said?" Conner asked.

"I did," I told him, swallowing hard. "And . . . we can't get back together."

Even with all of my thinking, and wise decision making—as wise as I knew it was—I had a hard time getting those words out, because Conner and I had been together a long time. And it was hard, you know, to choose to be alone.

But I learned some things while we were apart, I could survive without him, life went on without him, and I could actually have fun without him. I also learned I should live without him. He wasn't good enough for me.

Conner seemed dejected. But it sorta seemed as though he knew that would be my answer. "I really blew it, huh?" He set his jaw. "Can we still be friends, though?" He looked into my eyes. "Can we eat together? Maybe take things slow?"

I was surprised that he wanted to. I'd figured he would run back to Laura. Maybe he really had changed.

"Of course you can eat with us," I told him, glad that he wanted to. Glad that we might be able to salvage a friendship out of this mess. I hadn't really thought that was possible. But who knows, maybe it was. And if it was, that'd be great. And I'd try not to hold a grudge. I'd try super, super hard, like I'd make it a goal: forgive Conner—and his back-stabbing(s).

I wasn't sure what he meant by "take things slow," though. Was he saying he still hoped we might get back together someday? I wasn't sure how I felt about that.

But in any case, whatever he meant, he ate with Nina and me, and it was sort of like old times, but sort of not. I would never look at him the way I used to. He wasn't my hero anymore. He had let me down.

Still, I had to give him credit. He seemed to be trying to make up for past mistakes. It was nice. I was glad he was trying, glad he cared.

After school I had to work, but it was only a short shift. When I got home it was still early enough to call Trent—only it took me a long while to work up my nerve, because I knew he was going to turn me down cold. I knew it. The Deal was over. There was no reason he would feel obligated to help me out, especially when it was something I knew he didn't want to do. At all. Why bother asking? Why put myself through that kind of humiliation? But picturing Hailey's smug face gave me strength. I would beg him if I had to.

But when I called his house, he wasn't home. "Trent's working at Flips tonight," Mrs. Hayes said.

I quickly explained to Mom my urgent mission and sped to Flips. If I didn't ask Trent now, I never would, and if by the slightest chance he was miraculously willing to sing with me, we would need as much time as we could get to practice. There was no putting the question off until tomorrow.

When I got to Flips, Trent was talking with his band by the pool tables. His band. Yikes! I shoved my shyness aside. I didn't have time for it. I was on a mission. I hurried over to Trent.

"Can I talk to you for a second?"

Trent looked surprised to see me. "Sure."

His band went backstage to set up, and Trent gazed at me questioningly. "So, at lunch it looked as though the deal worked. Your boyfriend came back."

"Yeah," I said distractedly, trying to get the thoughts of Trent from the other night out of my head—thoughts of him holding me in his arms as we swayed to the music.

Focus, I ordered. You're on a mission.

I had to divert my gaze from Trent's alluring, brown eyes. Instead, I stared intently at his shirt. "I have a huge, gigantic favor to ask of you," I told it.

Trent seemed interested. "What?"

When I started explaining, he backed away, shaking his head with a smile. "I'm not singing with the Madrigals," he said before I had even fully explained.

"But you have to. Please! I need you. I *can't* let Hailey win. You have an amazing voice, Trent, and I have to win."

"Megan, I'm really sorry. I'd love to help you. I would. But I don't do show-tunes."

He started to walk away!

I was so desperate, I wanted to beg. But instead I got an idea. I grabbed a cue from off the wall. "Play me," I told him. "If I win, you'll sing with me."

Trent turned back, smiling. He looked intrigued.

He raised an eyebrow. "And if I win?"

"Whatever you want."

He thought for a moment, then his smile grew. "You'll sing with me. Right now. Tonight."

A chill ran through my body just hearing him say that. No way was I getting up on the stage in front of this crowd—our entire school, basically—and singing.

I swallowed. "You're on."

I watched him rack the balls, feeling uneasy. We have a pool table at home, and I'm pretty good—super good, really. I crush everyone who visits. So, I felt pretty confident I would win. But what if I didn't?

As we began to play, I started to sweat, realizing Trent was better than anyone who came to visit. I felt sick, realizing he might actually win.

And though the game was close, he *did* win.

Once he pocketed the eight-ball he stood smiling at me, looking every bit as smug as Hailey. "You're good."

"Yeah," I said through gritted teeth. "I'm a real champ."

He put away our cues, then smiled at me some more. "You ready?"

"Trent—I can't."

"Just do it like you did for me that night."

"I was a goof."

"You were great. Seriously." He took my hand. "Come on, before you chicken out."

"I *am* chickening out. I already have. Done deal."

"No, come on." He squeezed my hand. "I'll be with you, right next to you."

If I wasn't so nauseous at the thought of getting up on stage, this moment would have been mega, big-time romantic. No joke. His hand was so warm. And his words reassuring. But . . .

"I can't."

"Do it and I'll sing your show-tunes."

I blinked. "You'll do it?"

He tilted his head with a grin. "If you'll do it."

Trent led me up on stage, and I clung to his hand for dear life as he announced that I was going to sing. The crowd cheered as though I was cool, as though I was a star. It was nice.

But then Trent started to play his guitar and a wave of reality washed over me: I was up here to sing! I looked over at him, pleading for this to be a nightmare I could wake from. I even pinched myself.

Really hard. But the nightmare didn't go away.

Trent simply smiled encouragingly and kept playing, the rest of his band joining in. And when it was time for me to sing, I did. It didn't take any thought. None at all. It was my song, just with a little rock to it, and when my voice heard the music it wanted to sing, needed to sing. And I was up on stage, with lights shining on me, so what else could I do? I got into it, dancing without even consciously realizing I was doing it. And it was fun.

When the song was over, everyone cheered and cheered. Did I say those other nights were the best nights of my life? I was wrong. Totally wrong. Because this was!

chapter 22

After Baggage finished their performance, Trent followed me out to my car. I gave him sheet music and a tape with the accompaniment to the song we would be singing for the competition, called "Going the Extra Mile." It was a medley of a bunch of different show-tunes.

I smiled when he stared at the sheet music as though it were a skunk. "You aren't going to chicken out, are you?" I asked.

I was sort of afraid he would. I couldn't imagine him up on a stage singing this kind of song any more than he could. And there were the dance steps I'd coaxed Brian into doing and the suspenders and hat. But I wasn't going to mention any of that to Trent, at least not tonight.

Trent grimaced. "No. I'm not chickening out. We have a deal."

Relief. Happiness. "Okay, so look over the music and tomorrow—"

"You were really great tonight," Trent interrupted.

His earnest voice made me glad it was so dark out. Maybe he couldn't see that I was suddenly blushing crimson red. "It was fun," I murmured.

"I knew you would like it."

Just then Ed, the owner of Flips, stuck his head out the back entrance. "Trent are you out here?"

"Yeah," Trent called, looking back. "I'll be right there." He turned back to me, looking reluctant. "Well, I have to go."

But he didn't go. Instead, he tugged playfully on a lock of my hair and it seemed as though he was going to kiss me. My knees went wobbly with anticipation. I sort of *leaned in* with anticipation. But then, drat it, he didn't do it. Instead he backed away. "Well, see ya," he said.

Watching him go, I gave out a huge sigh. Of relief? Frustration? I wasn't sure. *Look,* I told myself impatiently, we've already had this conversation. A hundred times!!! He's not right for you. Get over him.

Right, I told myself, calling out to Trent, "We'll practice right after school."

"Right," he said as he went into Flips.

I sighed again, sad our deal was over. If it wasn't for my desperate need to have a duet partner, Trent probably would have never talked to me again. Knowing that weighed me down. But then I couldn't help looking on the bright side, Trent Ryan was going to do the duet with me!

*　*　*　*　*

Trent met me in the music room right after school. I'd been playing the piano, waiting. But, no joke, when I saw him walk into the room, I got goose bumps. True, honest-to-goodness goose bumps!

"Are you ready?" I asked with an enthusiastic smile.

Trent's smile wasn't as enthusiastic. But, hey, at least he smiled. Or maybe he grimaced. Whatever. "I guess."

I turned on the tape with the accompaniment, and only moments later, I was thrilled beyond words. It was obvious Trent had practiced. He had his part dead on, perfect. He made the funny parts funny, and the sad parts heart-wrenching. He put poor Brian to shame. And what was more important, we were good together, awesome.

It was as though Brian's moving away had been an answer to a prayer.

"This is fun, huh?" I coaxed Trent with a smile, after we'd been practicing for a while, tweaking perfection.

Trent grinned. "As long as no one from school sees us."

"Don't worry," I laughed. "No one comes to our performances. Only parents and old people. So," I couldn't go on with my request, though I really, truly wanted to. But I couldn't. It was too much to ask.

Trent looked at me quizzically. "So . . . what?"

"Well," I sighed, "You don't have to do it. We're super great, as is. Only, Brian and I, we sort of . . . *danced* a little while we sang."

Trent ran his hands through his hair, looking as though I'd just asked him to sing naked on stage. "You want me to do a dance?"

"Well, you don't *have* to," I told him.

Actually, I'd *made* Brian. But Brian and I needed the dance steps to add something to the song. Trent and I already had something, chemistry. As I said, we were awesome.

Still, I went on, despite Trent's horrified expression. "But they're really simple steps. Super easy. And they add so much."

I was excited. If I could possibly, possibly talk Trent into doing the steps we would not only win, we would go down in the books as the best duet in the history of Jefferson's honor choir.

Trent stared into my face as though begging me not to ask this of him. "You want me to sing this song—*and* do a dance?"

I laughed, as he made it sound as though the idea was inconceivable. "It would be really terrific and fun. Really."

"Okay," he said after a tormented moment. "I'm going to do it. Dance and sing. But you have to do me a favor in return."

I tilted my head. "A favor?" I would love to do him a favor! "What?"

"Sing again at Flips," he said. "This Friday. We'll advertise it and everything."

"Oh."

I would've loved to do him a favor, anything, practically, only . . . not that. Sure, it had been fun last night. But last night it had been on a whim. Doing it this way, planned out and advertised, no way! I would think about it too much, and get sick from worry.

But Trent was gazing at me with his sweet, puppy dog eyes. And he was going to wear a straw hat, and dance, and sing *show tunes* for me. How could I tell him no? "I—uh, guess."

I would have groaned about it for an hour, only we were going to practice the dance. He was actually going to do it! So, I grasped the opportunity while I could.

I taught him the steps, and as I said, they were super easy. But with him, they were kind of romantic, as they involved a lot of hugging and cuddling. I hadn't really noticed that with Brian. No wonder he had gotten the wrong idea about my intentions.

So, Trent and I danced and sang and it was super fun and a little romantic, and totally terrific. I could tell Trent was pleased, too. He even added some new steps. "This is kind of fun," he said. "You swear no one will see us?"

"No one will see us," I assured him. "But what if they did? Would that be so bad? We're really great, don't you think?"

He smiled, sort of rueful like, "Yeah. We're great."

* * * * *

Wednesday when I got to school, Nina ran up to me, smiling wide. "Looky," she said excitedly, shoving a flyer in my face.

Bewildered, I grabbed it. Then groaned, "No!"

It was a flyer for Flips, advertising me singing with Baggage this Friday. "Where did you *get* this?"

She grinned. "They're all over school."

"No!" I groaned again.

But they were. They were everywhere. And all day long people came up to me asking questions. When did I join the band? Would I be singing that song from Monday's performance? I would have enjoyed all of the attention. Really. If it hadn't made me so sick.

After school, when I met Trent in the music room, he blew off my nervous ranting with a smile. "You'll do great," he said. Then he eyed the outfit I held out for him, the one he'd be wearing for our duet. He raised his eyebrows. "If anyone should be nervous, it's me."

I smiled. "You'll do great."

Trent put on the straw hat, propping it on the side of his head. "Do I get a cane?"

I laughed. "Why? You want to hit me over the head with it?"

He grinned. "How did you know?" Then he sobered, changing the subject. "How are you and Conner doing?"

I looked down, knowing he must have seen that Laura and Conner were back together. Big shock there. "Let's practice," I said.

I knew I shouldn't be sad about Conner and Laura reuniting. I shouldn't care one way or the other. Unfortunately, my heart didn't care what it *should* do. It hurt. And I could tell that Trent felt sorry for me. That hurt too.

I wanted to ask about him and Caitlin. They sort of seemed back together, but sort of not. I couldn't bring it up, though. I was afraid I'd start bawling.

After practicing with Trent, I had to go to work. And when I got home, the house was empty. There was a note on the fridge from Mom, informing me she had gone home teaching with Dad. I looked through the fridge for a while, and then shut it without getting anything out. I was tired. Beat.

I had plans to fling myself across my bed. But when I got up to my room, there was a wrapped gift in the middle of it. What's this? I wondered excitedly, forgetting all about my exhaustion. Who could it be from? Trent? Or maybe its an apology from Conner?

I quickly read the card. "For Megan," was all it said.

Hmmm.

With lightening speed, I ripped open the gift. Then I sat, staring. Inside the box was a can of dog food.

chapter 23

"It was just Aspen," Nina assured me Thursday at school. "*She's* the one that needs dog food. The snake."

Though Aspen made it no secret that she hated me, I couldn't believe she would do this. Just thinking about it made me cringe. "She would've had to gone up to my room."

"Well, so would anyone else," Nina pointed out. "And who else could it be?"

I shrugged. Unfortunately, there *were* other choices. Even though Brian had moved away, Raven was still giving me dirty looks. And Caitlin wasn't exactly my biggest fan. Face it, I had a lot of enemies these days.

"Maybe it was Parker," I said, only thinking of him now because I saw him at his locker, scratching his armpit. "He's been belligerent ever since 'the car incident.'"

Nina smirked at the idea. "Yeah. He's waited around a whole *year* plotting his revenge, waiting until you least expected it."

I used to work with Parker at Limousine Pizza. For a while he and Nina dated, but then she had to dump him, as he was sort of a slime-ball. Parker didn't like that, being dumped. He started spreading filthy rumors about Nina. So one night, while he was in the store getting his next round of pizzas to deliver, I moved his car. I just parked it a few spaces down. Seriously, no big deal, but he came back in, screaming that it had been stolen. The whole store laughed, as they all knew what I'd done.

But Parker didn't take it well. He cursed me out until he was blue in the face. Everyone gave me high-fives. But I felt sort of bad. I

101

could tell Parker was majorly embarrassed. And although I'd *thought* I wanted to get him back, punish him for Nina, I found I didn't feel good about it. In fact, I felt guilty. Like I'd let someone down. Someone I was going to have to face tonight when I prayed.

So, even though it hurt (really, really bad), because I hated what he was doing to Nina, I apologized to Parker. But it was weird. He didn't take *that* well either. He seemed to think I was mocking him or something. I'm not sure. But he started swearing at me all over again. I just stood there in shock, with my jaw hanging open. He went on and on and on, ending his torrent with the threat, "I'll get you back, dog."

The words fit this situation, right?

I almost had myself convinced it *was* Parker, that he gave me the dog food. And for some reason it made me feel better thinking it was him. Why? I'm not sure, exactly. I guess because I'd actually done something to him. It made the act seem less vicious, petty even, like it was just a slime-ball getting lame revenge. Not someone who hated my guts for no reason.

Still, it creeped me out thinking he'd been in my room. Yuck!

Anyway, I was pretty convinced it was Parker that planted the sweet little gift. That is until Aspen and her friends walked by, barking. Then they all burst out laughing.

"Watch out or I'll call the dog catcher on you!" Nina called after them.

She gave me a sideways glance. "Guess it wasn't Parker."

"Guess not."

*   *   *   *   *

Tonight at work, I was unloading the morning's shipment, which I love to do. Seeing the brand new stuff always puts a little patter into my heart. Yeah, okay, I need to get a life. But I'd had a horrible yucky day, full of barking. I needed something to cheer me up. And new clothes were . . . uplifting.

"Wow," I said, opening the second box to find black leather

jackets. I stood in front of the full-length mirror, trying one on. *This would be so perfect for tomorrow*, I thought, posing.

I had no idea what to wear for the "Big Event." Nothing seemed right.

This would probably get too hot, though I told myself. Of course I could never, ever afford it, anyway. So it was all good.

"Excuse me."

I jumped at the unexpected voice. Then I hurriedly shoved the jacket back into the shipment box, saying, "Yes?" as crisp and business-like as possible. But it was hard because there stood Laura with Conner. And, let me tell ya, there's never been a face on earth that looked as smug.

"I'm looking for a formal dress," she informed me, wrapping her arm through Conner's. "I'm going to my boyfriend's sports banquet. He plays baseball." She said all this as though she had no clue who I was, which was just stupid. She'd *barked* at me earlier today.

But hearing that she was going to Conner's sports banquet gave a painful jab at my heart. I had gone with him last year, of course. We'd gotten into a who-can-eat-the-most-pie war. It had been fun.

But that was last year. A world ago.

"Formals are over there," I managed to choke out.

Conner looked back at me as Laura led him away. I didn't acknowledge his gaze, though. Instead, I went back to unpacking boxes. "At least I broke up with him this time," I thought. "So there!" In my mind, I stuck out my tongue in Laura's direction.

Actually, it made me feel better. Sorta.

As I was working, (or manhandling the shipment—whatever you want to call it) Jade, a co-worker and friend, sauntered over to me. "I think your customer could use a dressing room." She gestured to Laura who now had an armload of dresses, and was gathering more in record speed.

"She's *not* my customer," I growled.

Jade raised her eyebrows with surprise. "Am I sensing tension?"

"Little bit," I muttered. Then I took a deep breath, trying to summon up my good Mormon upbringing.

Not easy.

Still, I did my best.

On Sunday, Sister Green, my Laurel teacher, told us that when she gets upset with someone she has a trick. She plays that primary song, *Trying to be like Jesus*, in her head. She said it works. Helps calm her down. Gets her back in tune with the Spirit.

Well, let me tell ya, the Spirit had packed its bags and left the building. It was nowhere to be seen. Or heard. Or felt. So, out of desperation, I gave the song-in-my-head thing a shot. "I'm trying to be like Jesus. I'm following in his ways . . ."

Sigh.

Guess I couldn't call Laura names (out loud). I had to do that turn-the-other-cheek thing. But it was *hard*. She stole my boyfriend. Gave me dog food. Barked at me. Grrr!

Carry On, Carry On, Carry On!

I took a deep breath. "Look, I'm sure she's going to buy something ultra expensive," I told Jade. "You're welcome to the commission. Just watch your back."

"She's a real witch, huh?" Jade asked before going to help her.

"The *queen* of witches," I wanted to say. But didn't. Instead, I bit my tongue.

Jade looked back at me curiously, apparently wondering why I didn't answer.

So, I explained. "You know that saying? If you can't say something nice, don't say anything? Well, I'm doing that."

Jade nodded, smiling. "You go, girl."

My tongue hurt.

I went to the front register to ring up a customer, then finished some paper work. I saw Conner wandering toward me as Laura tried on dress after dress. When he came near the front counter, I walked away. He followed as I went from rack to rack, straightening.

"Look, stop following me," I told him. "And don't say you miss me, or us, or whatever, because I'm not going to listen to you anymore. You seem to be doing just fine without me."

"Yeah, well," Conner looked into my eyes, "things aren't always as they seem."

I gazed up at him, bewildered. He smiled ruefully. "Choose the Right, it's not as easy as it sounds."

"Conner," Laura called, "how do you like this one?"

Conner stared at me a moment. "Well, I have to go. But I'm going to come hear you sing tomorrow."

I watched him walk away, for some stupid reason feeling as though I might cry. But I was getting over him. Really. I knew it, because I felt more sorry for him than myself.

chapter 24

Trent drove up on Friday afternoon as I was cleaning out the garage.

"You ready?" he asked.

I tilted my head, wiping sweat off my brow. "Ready for what?"

"To practice *The Road Home* with the band."

He said it as though I should know what he was talking about, but I didn't. When he called earlier, he'd said we would practice "before the show." So of course I thought we would practice tonight—*before the show*. Not right now. Obviously.

"Well, I have to change," I told him. *And take a shower, and put on make up, and do my hair,* I inwardly listed.

Trent shook his head. "There's not time. The guys have to work. Just bring the dress. You can change there, before we go on."

"Uh . . . okay," I said hesitantly, unable to protest, although I wanted to. Desperately. I hadn't even decided what I was going to wear yet. And I wanted to look super nice for tonight. Not like I'd just cleaned my garage. But the whole band was sitting in Trent's car, waiting for me. What could I do?

I scrambled upstairs, grabbed one of the dresses I'd thought about wearing (actually, it made the decision way easier), and plastered on deodorant. Then I undid my pony, fluffed my hair out a bit and miracles of miracles—it looked really good.

"Thank you!" I gasped.

I coated it with hairspray, grabbed some lip-gloss, and was out the door, like lightening, sorta.

* * * * *

I practiced with Baggage. And to my surprise, they were all super nice guys.

"You have an awesome voice," they told me.

And they complimented my song and treated me as though I was one of them, a musician. It was cool, especially because I'd always looked up to them. Like idols.

After practice, they gave me a free hamburger and fries.

"Do you have any more songs?" asked Mike, the super cute drummer, as he brought me another soda.

I blinked. "Yeah. I have lots."

"Cool," he said. "Welcome to the band."

My feet tapped a spastic jig under the table. I was part of the band!!! Cool!

When the guys had to go to work—waiting tables and flipping pizzas—I played air hockey with Nina, trying to occupy my brain—keep it from thinking about later, when I'd have to get up on stage in front of the whole school. Because, basically, the whole school was here. Yikes!

"Don't look," Nina groaned.

There was Laura and Aspen. They were sitting in a booth with their friends. When the two saw me, they smiled conspiratorially at each other. It made me feel funny. What was that about? More plans to bark at me?

"My biggest fans," I muttered.

"Yeah," Nina said. "And they're holding their fan club meeting right here. How lucky." She eyed me worriedly. "Don't let them get to you, Megan. That's what they want."

I nodded. "I know."

I tried ignoring them, but it was hard. Why'd they have to be here? Why'd they have to ruin *everything*? I mean, what was the matter with them? Why were they so evil?

Why'd they hate me so much?

By the time I had to get dressed, I was sweating. Not just because of Laura and Aspen. The place was packed. I don't know if it had to do with the flyers or not. Friday nights were always busy at Flips. But to me the place seemed even busier than usual.

I hurriedly grabbed my dress off the hook. Then I stopped, cold. My dress! I gazed at it in horror, not believing my eyes. It was ruined! Someone had attacked it with a knife or scissors or something. My beautiful dress was slashed to ribbons.

I couldn't believe it.

Who could have done this? But the moment I asked, I knew the answer—Laura and Aspen. No wonder they had looked so pleased with themselves. Monsters!

I bit my lip, trying to calm down.

What could I do?

I was supposed to be out on stage in a couple of minutes. But no way was I going up there dressed like this. I was still in my cleaning-out-the-garage gear. What could I do? There was no time to go home and grab something else.

I was sunk.

Desperate, I scrambled out into Flips, trying to remember what Nina had been wearing. Was it something cool? I passed Aspen and Laura. They both broke out laughing when they saw me, but I didn't have time to care. It was a blur. Where was Nina?

The first person I ran into was Audrey Tolley, from church. She, of course, was dressed like a fashion model. She was *always* dressed like a fashion model.

The outfit was perfect. But the thing was, could I get her to switch with me? She came with a hot guy she was crushing on and I was wearing smelly cleaning-out-the-garage clothes.

"What's the matter?" Audrey asked when I swooped up on her all end-of-the-world like.

"Sure, I'll trade with you," she said as soon as I told her what happened. There wasn't even any needing-to-think-about-it type pause. Of course, with her body she could probably make my dumpy sweats look like they belonged on a catwalk.

We finished the swap, and I was smoothing down my new skirt, just as Trent announced me. I went out onto stage with 10,000 trillion butterflies storming through my stomach. The crowd went wild, cheering. But to my horror, some of them *barked*.

"Great," I muttered.

But in a way, the barking was good. Just what I needed. Because I sorta found a rebellious streak in me. Hearing the barks, the butterflies flew away. Suddenly, I had something to prove. When the music started I belted out my song with everything I had. No way was I going to let Laura and Aspen and their mangy friends get the best of me. I was through playing that game.

chapter 25

Saturday morning as I was getting ready to go over to Trent's to practice for our duet, Conner called. "You were great last night," he said.

I smiled, pleased that he'd been there. 'Cause I'd rocked.

"Sorry about Laura and Aspen," he said. "And all of their stupid friends."

For the briefest of moments, I thought about telling him what they had done to my dress, but decided not to. I didn't have time to go into a long discussion of how rotten Laura was. If he couldn't see it by now, well, then he was blind and stupid.

"Thanks for calling," I told him. "But I've got to run."

I hung up without shedding a single tear or even thinking about shedding one. No trauma. No drama. No nothing. *You've come a long way, baby!* I told myself.

When I got to Trent's, he answered the door, leading me into his kitchen where he was making cookies. Which, in itself, was a shock. Who knew Trent Ryan could bake?

"They're a treat for after we practice," he said, as he pulled out a dozen cinnamony beauties from the oven. "Because I have something to tell you."

Hearing that would have been big news to me, only I'm easily distracted by cookies. Instead of picking up on the seriousness in his voice, I exclaimed, "Oh! Snickerdoodles! My favorite!"

He grinned, reminding me, "They're for *after* practice."

As I watched him slide the Snickerdoodles onto the cooling rack, I noticed something (which is kind of remarkable, since there were cookies right in front of me). He had on a CTR ring!

"Hey, you have a CTR ring!" I exclaimed.

He gave it an appreciative glance. "Yeah, it stands for Choose The Right," he explained. The way he said it, it was as though I had never seen such a ring. It was cute.

He went on, "Most of the kids in our class have one. So, of course, Wendy wanted one, too. Then while I was there, at the church store, I thought I might as well get myself one." He bit his lip. "You know, as a reminder not to drink and stuff."

I stared up at him in amazement. He was full of surprises, special, wonderful surprises. Who was this boy that took over Trent Ryan's body?! I *loved* him.

Trent grinned, raising an eyebrow quizzically. "Why are you looking at me like that?"

Because I love you, I wanted to tell him—but of course I didn't. Instead, I said, "You have a little cookie-dough on your chin." I reached up to him, rubbing the lie away with my finger.

Trent watched me as I did it, and he got that "look." The one he gets sometimes. That dreamy, "Come hither and be mine," expression. I thought he was going to kiss me. It seemed as though he was going to. I held my breath, thinking: finally!

But of course he didn't kiss me. He *never* kissed me. It was my stupid rule. Stupid, stupid rule! Instead he cleared his throat, backing away. "Are you ready?" he said.

Trent led me down to his basement. It was finished and full of musical instruments. "This is the music room," he said, walking to the little refrigerator in the corner of the room. "Do you want something to drink?"

Holding my breath, I peeked into the little fridge. Then I smiled, warmed. There wasn't a beer in it, not one. Just sodas. Gobs and gobs of sodas. Sweet soda! *Wonderful* soda! Maybe that night when he went down to the basement to get himself and Caitlin "drinks" he didn't get them beers after all. Maybe he got them one of these sodas. It was possible. More than possible, really. It was like, probably. After all, this was his basement, and this was the only fridge down here and it was stocked with: SODA!!!

"No thanks," I said, twirling around in the massive space, loving the room. It was like a music store right in his house. But then I noticed something. The store was void of customers, namely, Wendy.

"She's at dance lessons," Trent said when I asked. "We're alone. Is that okay?"

I reddened. "Sure." It wasn't as though I thought he was going to attack me or anything. But things were suddenly sort of awkward.

He watched me. "It's just I wanted us to talk alone after we practice, okay?"

"Sure," I said, trying to sound breezy. Only I wasn't breezy. I was suddenly worried. What did he want to talk to me about? And why did he need us to be alone for it? Was he going to say something horrible? Something that would make me cry?

I would have supposed he was going to tell me he'd decided not to sing the duet with me, only he was waiting until *after* the practice to tell me. So, I was pretty sure that wasn't it.

"Wh—what is it we're going to talk about?" I asked. Lately, he'd been acting funny. Like he wanted to tell me something, only he kept chickening out. Remembering that suddenly knotted my stomach. It had to be something terrible, horrible even, to turn *Trent* into a chicken.

"After we practice," he said.

So, we practiced. Practiced, practiced, practiced. But the thing was, we were great. Terrific. We were so incredibly awesome I couldn't help jumping up and down and generally being a spaz.

"Don't you think we're fantastic?" I said, trying to get Trent a little spazzy too.

"Yeah." He smiled ruefully. "We're great."

Why'd he seem so sad about it?

I tilted my head. "So what were you going to tell me?" I asked. He started to hesitate, so I interjected, "Tell me now or I'll die!"

Trent bit his lip, seeming anxious. The knot in my stomach tightened. What could possibly be so terrible?

"Let's go upstairs," he said. "Have a cookie. Snickerdoodles, your favorite."

I followed him upstairs and let him pour me a glass of milk to go with my cookies. "Okay," I said, my stomach a tangled ball of knots. "What is it?"

Trent sat down beside me, looking uneasy. "Why do you think I like you so much?"

I blinked. "Do you like me so much?"

"Gee, Megan, what does it take? I took you to the dance. I'm singing goofy show-tunes for you and dancing a jig. I'm even taking missionary lessons so I can be the kind of guy you like. What do you think? Maybe I like you, a little bit?"

Suddenly my heart was pounding so hard I was sure it was going to pounce right out of my chest. He was taking missionary lessons?! He liked me?! HE WAS TAKING MISSIONARY LESSONS?

I gulped down my milk, almost choking on it. "You're taking missionary lessons?"

"Yeah. I had a bunch of questions in Mrs. Springsteed's class. She had me make an appointment with the missionaries. Wendy and I, we're on the third discussion."

I couldn't help the gigantically huge smile plastered on my face. I didn't even try to control it. "Trent, that's so great!"

Trent ran his hands through his hair, still looking uneasy. "Yeah, but why did I come to your church in the first place? Why was I so attracted to you?"

"You were attracted to me?"

"Yeah, Megan, I was attracted to you. I never made it a secret. Why is all of this a surprise to you?"

"I don't know. I thought you were messing around."

Trent shook his head, staring at me intently. "I'm not messing around."

He stared into my eyes. "I'm completely serious."

He went on. "But why? Why do you think I like you so much?"

"My . . . hair?" I do have sort of nice hair. It's definitely my best feature. Not that it's perfect. A lot of times it's like a wild beast I can't control. But it's long and full. If I were to cut it short I don't think a guy would look at me twice. Needles to say, I have no plans to cut it.

Trent grinned. "Yeah, that's it. Your hair. It's all I can think about. It keeps me up at night." His eyes danced with amusement. "Your hair's great. It is. But that's not it. It's *you*, Megan. I like you."

Hearing him keep saying that was getting me delirious. I needed to change the subject before I started doing cartwheels or something.

"It was Caitlin you did this for," I reminded him. Then I went on to tell him what I'd suspected all along, wanting him to know I was profoundly wise and understood what he was going through. "You have deep, ambiguous feelings for her."

"What?" Trent looked at me as though I was nuts. "I don't have 'feelings' for Caitlin. I feel bad for her. I want to shake her and tell her she's screwing up her life. But I don't have 'feelings' for her."

I looked at him skeptically, and he relented. "Well, I guess at one time I *thought* I did, but that was a long time ago, before I got to know her." Trent ran his hands through his hair. "See, that's what happens all the time. I think I like a girl until I get to know her. But with you it was different. With you—"

Right then Wendy came bounding through the front door. "Megan!" she exclaimed, rushing to give me a hug.

"Hi, Wendy." I hugged her back, noticing their Mom standing in the doorway, smiling at us. "Hello," I said to her. "I'm Megan Turner."

The woman looked a little puzzled. "Megan Turner? Why does that sound so familiar?—and you look familiar. Do I know you from somewhere?" Then she seemed to piece it all together. "Oh, I know. You're the girl I bought Charlie's computer from."

I stood staring at her, now recognizing her as well. "Yeah," I said in astonishment. "It's good to see you again Mrs. Hayes."

She smiled glancing at the heaping plate of Snickerdoodles on the table. "You brought Charlie cookies?"

I shook my head, still slightly dazed. This was too incredible.

Trent's mom was the lady that bought my old computer, the one Conner had helped me sell? I remembered she had said she was buying it to surprise her son for his Birthday. Trent was her son?! Trent *owned* my old computer?!

"Trent made them," I told her, referring to the Snickerdoodles.

Mrs. Hayes seemed amazed. "Charlie made you cookies? That's a first." She smiled and gave me a wink. "He must like you a lot."

Trent put his hand on my shoulder. "I do."

Mrs. Hayes looked surprised by her son's candor. "Well . . ."

Trent didn't wait for her to go on with that thought. Instead, he steered me toward the door. "I'll walk you to your car," he said.

I looked back at him questioningly. I hadn't been planning to leave, not for a long time. But he was hurrying me out the door as though the house was on fire.

"My cookies!" I said.

Trent relented. "Okay, wait by your car and I'll get them."

I gave him a look that said, "What in the Sam Hill is going on?"

Trent played with a lock of my hair. "Just do it, okay?" he said gently. "I need to talk to you—alone."

He waited until I walked all the way to my car before he went back into the house.

Boy, he was acting weird! But he liked me, and he was taking missionary lessons! Nothing he had to say could possibly be bigger than that. So I waited by my car with tickles in my stomach and a song in my heart. It went like this: He likes me! He likes me! He like, like, like, likes me!

When Trent came out he was carrying a gallon-sized baggie of snickerdoodles. And I guess he gave up on breaking his horrible news to me gently. I guess he decided the best approach was to simply plunge the knife into my heart in one brutal jab.

He handed me the cookies saying, "I read your computer."

My smile froze. "What?"

"Your hard drive. It was recoverable. I read it."

"No!" I backed away from him.

"Megan," he put his hand on my shoulder, but I shook it away.

Now I understood. Understood how he knew so much about me. Understood how this whole fraudulent, fantasy came into existence. He read the files off my computer. The jerk read my journal!

chapter 26

What a dope I had been! A sap. All of this, this whole time, it had all been Trent's big *joke*. He read my journal. He knew everything about me. He knew exactly how to push my buttons, and he had! He'd pushed them all. Every one.

I was a moron!

I bolted to my car, but Trent grabbed my arm. "Megan, wait a minute. Let me explain."

I pushed him away. "I hate you!" I sobbed.

I got into my car and tore out of his driveway, heading down the street. But I was a shaking mess, a wreck waiting to happen. As soon as I rounded the corner, I pulled over and bawled my eyes out.

When I finally got home, I flung myself across my bed, still bawling. How stupid I had been this afternoon. When Trent told me he was taking the missionary lessons my heart had raced with happiness. "Yes!" I'd thought. "Now we can date."

But he'd only been playing some bizarre, cruel joke. (The kind "cool" people from Jefferson play. The kind I never got.) He probably laughed about me with Caitlin and his friends. Constantly. Continually.

"Guess how I messed with Megan The Mormon's head today," he'd say. "Today I made her think I was interested in her church." Or, crueler yet, "Today I made the pathetic sap think I'm interested in *her*!"

Imagining the traumatic scene made me sob even harder. What a moron I had been! Megan the Mormon moron.

* * * * *

Sunday, Trent and Wendy came to church again.

When I saw them walk in, I spun back around in my seat, practically giving myself whiplash. Suddenly I was all sweaty.

"Why is he bothering to go on with this?" I wondered, my face growing hot with anger and shame. "Why doesn't he just leave me alone now? Move on to someone else?"

I had to wipe away a tear. And I hated that. That he got to see me cry. I refused to do it again. Ever. He was a jerk. A bully. He wasn't worth my tears. I wanted to forget him. Now. Forget everything that happened. None of it had been real anyway. It had all been an act, every last bit of it. *Guess how I messed with Megan The Mormon's head today.*

After sacrament meeting, Trent and Wendy came up to me as I was waiting for Nina in the hall. "Just stay away from me," I growled, storming off. But after I did it, I felt miserable. Poor Wendy. She'd looked hurt, stunned. She was completely innocent of Trent's mean game. I hated that I'd hurt her. I wanted to go back and apologize. Explain that I hadn't meant to be cruel to *her*. But I couldn't find the strength to go back and look for them. Actually, I didn't want to see either of them ever again.

But all through Sunday school, I couldn't get Wendy's hurt face out of my head. I had to apologize.

After church, I waited for her outside of her primary class. When she came out, I focused on her, only her. "Wendy, can I talk to you?" Then I glared at Trent. "Alone?"

I took her aside and said I was sorry for acting so mean. "I was mad at your brother, not you."

"I know." Wendy smiled. "Charlie explained that you two are in a misunderstanding."

A misunderstanding?! He called it a *misunderstanding*?!

Trent grabbed my arm, pulling me aside. "Now, I want to talk to you, alone." I tried to pull away, but he tightened his grip. "Just let me explain."

People were watching us, looking concerned. Sister Somebody furrowed her brow. "Is everything all right?"

"No!" I said, glaring at Trent.

He let go of my arm. "I just want to talk to you."

"Well, I don't want to talk to *you*," I told him, and stormed away.

chapter 27

Today in third period Ms. Wright was doing something weird. "Experimental."

"I've been teaching most of you all year," she said as soon as everyone was seated. "But it's only an hour a day, and I want to get to know you. Really know you. But more importantly, I want you to get to know yourselves."

Ms. Wright explained that she had a top hat full of questions, personal questions, and she was going to pull them out one by one. She was going to go around the room, asking each of us a different question. A question we would have to answer. Aloud.

"I want you to answer them honestly," she said. "So take your time. Really think about your answers."

Ms. Wright pulled out the first question, assigning it to Shawna, since Shawna sat at the front of the class. It made me glad I was sort of toward the back.

Ms. Wright read, "If you were the president of the United States, what policy, big or small, would you change?"

I slunk down in my seat only half-listening to Ms. Wright's unrelenting questions and each student's wavering answers, wishing I hadn't come to class today. After all, I was feeling kind of sick. And this "getting to know you" thing wasn't going to make me feel any better. I hated stuff like this. Stuff where I had to . . . talk. Of course it would happen in *this* class, with snotty Aspen and slime-ball Trent.

When it was my turn to answer a question, I slumped down in my seat, trying to be invisible. "Megan," Ms. Wright said, "If you could be anyone in the world, who would you be?"

That was easy. "Taylor Scott," I said.

When everyone looked at me like, who? I went on to explain, "He's this awesome composer and I'm trying to write this song that's kind of like his and," I just went on and on, my face growing sizzling hot, all the while wishing I had simply answered Lindsay Lohan.

When it was Trent's turn, he had been reading a magazine. I don't think he had a clue what was going on. Ms. Wright asked him, "Trent, what's dear to you?"

"Megan Turner," he answered without a moment's hesitation. Then he went on reading his magazine.

I stared at him in disbelief. Everyone else ooohed and aahhed.

Why'd he *say* that? Why was he doing this?

I stared down at my hands for the rest of class, ignoring Nina's gaze. When class was over, Nina put her hand on my shoulder. "Are you okay?"

I shook my head, ready to cry. Guys were jerks. All of them. They made you trust them, believe in them, but it always ended the same, with a big sharp knife in your back.

A tear ran down my cheek. "He knows everything, Nina. My dorky crush on him, us making him all those cookies. This whole time that he's been acting so nice, he's just been laughing at me."

"He sounded serious," Nina said. "About that what's dear to him thing."

"He wasn't serious!" I groaned. "He's just playing games. This is all a big joke to him. He's a jerk. I hate him."

After class, Caitlin was at my locker. "Hey, Megan," she said awkwardly. "I know we aren't exactly friends. But Trent *is* my friend. And he's really down. I don't know exactly what happened between you. I mean, you're fighting, but Trent, he really likes you and—"

"Look, just drop the act," I snapped. "I know you guys were in this together. A big laugh on Megan The Mormon, good one. But it's over, okay? Just knock it off and leave me alone."

I stormed away without getting my books for fourth. It didn't matter anyway. No way could I concentrate on math theorems. What was Trent doing to me? Why was he being so horrible? What did he think he would accomplish by sending Caitlin to talk to me? Caitlin! Did he actually believe I would listen to a word she had to say? Did he really think I was that gullible?

During pre-calculus Brooke Hunter slipped me a note. It read: *It was so sweet of Trent to say you were dear to him—right in front of the whole class. Romantic!!! You two make a cute couple.* Then she had drawn a smiley face.

I wadded up the note and threw in the wastebasket. The whole school was gullible.

chapter 28

Tuesday, after Ms. Wright's class, Trent ambushed me. He blocked me against my locker, forcing me to listen to him. "I didn't know it was yours," he said. "I had no idea." He ignored my attempts to push him away. "Listen, how could I possibly know? My mom said she got the computer off eBay."

"Off eBbay *local*," I snapped.

"Well, she didn't tell me that. She just said eBay, and so it could have come from anywhere. And it was just fun—and I thought totally harmless—to read about this cool chick that liked to write songs."

I looked away.

"Look, I was going to tell you about the computer. It was just— the moment never seemed right." Trent made me look up at him. "Megan, I was trying to tell you Saturday at my house. That's what my big talk was about, explaining why I'd been so drawn to you before I actually knew you. It was because I *did* know you. I knew everything about you."

"I don't want to hear this!" I pushed him away. "You had no right to know everything about me."

I stormed off to class with the words, "I didn't know it was yours!" trailing after me.

I hated Trent! *Hated* him. I wanted to disappear. Him to disappear. He had read my most intimate thoughts and feelings. He knew everything.

* * * * *

In chemistry we had a sub. So no lab, thank goodness. If I'd had to work with chemicals I probably would have blown up the whole school making banana oil. As it was, I sat all through class writing: I hate Trent Ryan. I hate Trent Ryan. I wrote it on my notebook over and over again. I hate Trent Ryan.

But then, all of a sudden, I remembered something, and it made me feel kind of sick. This morning in seminary, our teacher, Brother Shelton, had challenged us to spend the day pretending Heavenly Father came to school with us. "Because He does, everyday," Brother Shelton said.

I imagined Heavenly Father peeking over my shoulder now, seeing what I was working on. Man! I quickly scribbled out the words.

I was going to need a new notebook.

After school, Trent was leaning against my car. He just wouldn't go away. "What do you want?" I tried not to growl, but I think I did.

"Look, I know you're mad at me and in a way, you have every right to be. But I didn't know it was you."

"For how long?" I snapped. "The first paragraph? The third entry? When? Because I know you had to have figured it out before you came up with your great 'deal.'"

Trent bit his lip. "Yeah. I knew before that."

"So, just stay away from me," I told him, getting into my car.

"What about practicing for the duet?"

"Forget the duet. I don't care about the duet anymore," I told him. And I didn't, for the most part. I mean, I still would have liked to beat Hailey. But there were many things I would have liked more, like Trent not being a big, fat fake, or Trent stuffing his head in a toilet. Things like that.

"Won't you just listen to me?" Trent said. "Just let me explain?"

"No," I told him flatly. "I'm never going to listen to another word you have to say."

*   *   *   *   *

When I got home from work tonight there was an e-mail waiting for me from Trent.

> Megan, you have to understand, when I first started reading I didn't know it was your computer. I had no idea. I just liked the girl I read about. I thought it would be cool to get to know her. But I didn't dream it was someone I actually knew. Even when I read all the Mormon stuff. It just made me interested in your church.
>
> But see, this girl—her brother died, and it was comforting to hear her thoughts about that, because, you know, my dad died. She was so certain she would see her brother again. It made me feel comforted. Like maybe I could see my dad again, too.
>
> And this girl—she was so amazing. She was sweet, and made up cool songs and poems. And she was everything I wanted. But for all I knew, she lived in Australia. Besides, she had a boyfriend. I was seriously jealous of that guy. I figured he had to be cool beyond cool to have a girl like that. But see, Megan, I didn't put it together. The guy's name was *Cody*, and your boyfriend's name was Conner. . ..

I stopped reading, sitting back in my chair. Did I really want to go on? His words were doing things to my heart—twisting it inside out.

I should just stop, I told myself. Be an Ice Queen.

But, of course, being me, I read on.

It wasn't until I got to the part of the journal about the girl's summer, reading that she got a job as a counselor at Sunshine Day Camp (Wendy's day camp) that I actually started to put it together. The girl went on and on about the sweetest little camper named Wendy.

And that was it.

Figuring it out—that my fantasy girl was Megan-The-Mormon, Miss Goodness and Light— I didn't know what to do. It didn't seem possible.

Dazed, I went on reading. Because I couldn't really believe it—that I actually *knew* the girl I'd been reading about—dreaming about.

Seriously. It just couldn't be possible.

Then I got to the part where I gave you Wendy's gift. And you wrote about the eighth grade—back when you and Nina made me the infamous peanut butter cookies.

"Oh, no!" I groaned, almost falling out of my chair. Somehow I had hoped beyond hope that he hadn't read that—that he hadn't gone on. After all, he'd figured out who I was. He should have stopped!

"Big jerk," I muttered, reading on.

That's when I stopped reading the journal. Because then I knew for sure—it was yours. Megan The Mormon's. I felt like a creep. I didn't know what to do. Apologize? I couldn't do that. I figured it would just embarrass you. And me. I decided the best thing to do was just avoid you. Leave you alone.

Only that was really hard. Because now that I knew it was your journal, I sort of had a huge crush on you. I mean it, all I could do was think about you. And then when Aspen was giving you a hard time in class about the dance—I couldn't help it, I just blurted it out—that I would take you. Then I sat there for the rest of class trying to convince myself I'd only done it to help you out. "It's the least I can do for her," I told myself. "After all, I read her *journal*."

And while I was at it, I figured I could help you get your boyfriend back too. After all, I'd read how much you loved him. He'd obviously made a mistake and just needed to realize it . . . so I thought I'd help.

I figured "The Deal" was the way to go. And I figured it could help me out as well. I mean, I had this "thing" for you. And I didn't know what to do about it. I figured I could get over you faster if I was around you a lot. See, that's how I usually get over a girl—just hang around her. Get to know her. But it was different with you, Megan. The more I was around you, the more I liked you.

chapter 29

After reading Trent's e-mail I sat back, trying to absorb everything it said.

Okay. I'm not made of stone. And any walls I tried to build to guard myself against Trent were crumbling. But I couldn't forgive him. I couldn't! He knew my innermost thoughts. He knew everything about me. Everything!

And I was still mad. 'Cause he'd acted like he didn't know—didn't know about the peanut butter cookies, or my huge, idiotic crush on him—when he knew. Totally knew. It was embarrassing, humiliating, demoralizing—*unforgivable*.

Every day I would see Trent in class and every day I would turn away from him. But every night he would send me a new e-mail. Every night.

Tuesday night:

The thing about you and Conner was, I thought you guys would get back together. The way you wrote about your relationship—it sounded like love. I mean, you made this Cody sound like a great guy. I thought he deserved you. But he doesn't deserve you. The guy's a dope.

But, at the time, I didn't know that. All I had to go by was the great impression you left of him in your computer. So,

I thought the guy had messed up—for a minute. And then when Aspen started giving you a hard time, I thought maybe I could help you out—you know, let him see what he gave up.

But spending time with you—it let me see that I'm not a dope like your ex-boyfriend. I'm not giving up, Megan. I can't give you up.

Wednesday night:

Remember how I said I used to get over a girl I thought I liked?—just get to know her? Well, I'm serious. That's all it ever took. But it's different with you, Megan. I like you *because* I know you.

Thursday night:

Megan, I can't really say that I'm sorry I read your journal, because I'm not. That was how I got to find out who you were. And I'm not sorry I found that out. I'm only sorry that it hurt you. For that, I am truly sorry.

* * * * *

By Friday I wasn't especially mad anymore. Embarrassed, definitely. But mad, not so much. I really wanted to talk to Trent. But he wasn't in third period. Seeing his empty seat made me feel funny—sad. Why wasn't he here?

Ms. Wright was handing out a quiz on the film we watched yesterday when an announcement came over the school's intercom:

"Excuse me, I have an important announcement to make and I

have to hurry because I'm going to get suspended for this—but it's worth it."

I sat up, knowing that voice. It was Trent!

He went on, "This is for a girl that I care about a lot, but I hurt her really bad, and I'm so sorry that I'm going crazy. So I wrote her this—"

Then he *sang*:

"Megan the Mormon I'm sorry I hurt you so bad. It troubles me deeply that I made you sad. If you forgive me dear Megan, I'll do anything you want. Even immerse in a baptismal font."

Hearing that, I stood up. "Yes!"

The whole class gazed up at me with surprise—I'm usually pretty quiet. Like a mouse. And we were in the middle of a quiz. But everyone was smiling—cheering for me. Everyone but Aspen.

"Can I be excused?" I asked Ms. Wright.

She smiled. "By all means."

I ran out of class and headed for the office. But when I got there, I could see Trent getting chewed out by our principle, Mr. Peterson. I wanted to give Trent a little wave—a sign of some sort, to let him know that I wasn't mad anymore. But Mrs. Rogers, the office-lady, shooed me away. "Go back to class before you get into trouble, too," she said.

There wasn't anything I could do. Not that I could think of anyway. So, I slunk back to class. And took my quiz. And got a 100 percent. (It didn't involve chemicals.)

At lunch, I heard that Trent had been suspended for the rest of the day. That made me so sad. I felt bad. Super bad.

"It's my fault he's in trouble," I told Nina miserably. "If I'd just forgiven him earlier, he wouldn't have made that announcement."

Nina grinned. "But it was a great announcement." Her smile broadened. "Every girl in school is jealous of you."

That didn't really make me feel much better. But it did some. Well, actually, a lot.

When I got home from school, I tried calling Trent, but his step-dad answered. "Trent can't talk," he said. "That boy is in trouble."

I hung up with a new wave of guilt washing over me.

Poor Trent!

Tonight was the big "Honor Choir Competition" but now I didn't even want to go. I wanted to stay home and mope, eat a lot of chocolate, and wallow in guilt and despair. But I couldn't do that to the other Madrigals. I would sing in the choir. I just wouldn't do a duet, obviously.

*   *   *   *   *

On the way to the competition, I rode in the back seat of my parent's car, sighing. A lot. I know I'd told Trent I didn't care about the duet anymore. But I did! Now that it was here, I cared a lot. A whole lot. I couldn't bear watching Hailey win *again*. Not again! Life was too cruel. Unjust. Unfair!

Mom gazed back at me as we pulled into Roosevelt's parking lot. "Honey, are you feeling okay?"

"No! I'm sick! Take me back home!" I wanted to wail. But I didn't. Instead, I sighed (again). "I'm fine," I said, slipping out of the car.

When the competition started, Madrigals were on first. We did an outstanding job, just as I knew we would. Unfortunately, all the honor choirs do an outstanding job. That's why it's "honor choir."

I saw Hailey file onto the stage with the rest of her class. But behold! Her heels were unbelievable, mega-high, death-traps. She kind of wobbled as she climbed the stairs. I held my breath, watching a moment, positive she was going to stumble. Land on her rear-end.

It was weird. In my head, I could picture it clearly, as though it was real. But in true life it didn't seem to be in the cards. She took her place, safe and sound.

Sigh.

Oh well, it's for the best, I tried telling myself.

If she had tripped, I would have felt guilty, like I willed it to happen. And I had enough guilt on my plate, enough to last a lifetime. I couldn't choke down any more.

So, blasting the primary song *I'm Trying to be Like Jesus* in my head, I tried to be glad Hailey didn't trip. Glad she would get to do her duet. Only, sometimes it's hard being like Jesus. And other times it's super hard.

Times like this. (Times when my evil, singing nemesis was destined to win yet again!) Still, I did my best because, you know, it's the Mormon way. Carry On, Carry On, Carry On!

I was getting ready to go sit with my parents, when there was a tap on my shoulder. I turned around to find my knight in shinning armor, only he was wearing suspenders and a straw hat.

"Trent!" I exclaimed, hardly able to believe my eyes.

He came!

Trent tipped his hat. "Am I too late?"

I stared at him in wonder, my heart pounding like a jackhammer. We were going to do it after all?! We were going to sing our duet?!

"No! You're not too late," I told him excitedly, finding it hard not to do cartwheels and flips and other various acrobats—my heart sure was. "You're just in time. Come on!" I rushed him over to introduce him to Mr. Smith. "Can we still do our duet?" I asked, barely able to stand still.

Mr. Smith seemed pleased. "I'll go add your names to the program," he said, hurrying away.

I stared at Trent, still wide-eyed. "I can't believe your parents let you come."

Trent grinned. "Are you kidding? When I told them about it, they ran to the car. They're taking movies. I guess they know that's worse punishment than being suspended."

I laughed, pulling his hat down over his face. "Poor guy."

"Yeah. No kidding." Trent adjusted his hat. Then he gazed at me. "So are you still mad?"

I shook my head.

Trent widened his eyes. "You forgive me?"

I nodded.

He played with a lock of my hair. "I'm sorry I hurt you."

Hearing the earnestness in his voice, not to mention *seeing* it in his warm, brown eyes, melted my already softened heart.

Besides, everything worked out for the best. Everything worked out wonderful.

If Trent hadn't read my journal he would have never gotten to know me. And I, in turn, would have never gotten to know him. Not the real him. The one that was standing before me, full of "Goodness and Light." It's true what they say, the Lord works in mysterious ways.

"Are you really going to get baptized?"

He raised his eyebrows matter-of-factly. "I know this church is true," he said, saying it as though he was up on the stand, bearing his testimony.

I was so overcome with happiness, I attacked him with a ferocious hug, practically knocking him to the ground. Well, not really. He didn't almost fall to the ground. But he would have if he wasn't such a strong, hunky guy. If he wasn't so manly. If he was ten.

I noticed Hailey staring at Trent and me from across the room. She looked worried, as though she knew we were going to rock. As though she could tell just by looking at us that we were a force to be reckoned with: a winning couple. I smiled at her, trying not to look *too* smug.

Just then our names were announced.

Trent smiled. "Are you ready?"

"Yeah," I said with a grin, and we went out on to the stage holding hands, ready to sing the perfect duet.

about the author

Melanie Marks was born and raised in California. She is married to a naval nuclear submarine officer, and blessed with three amazingly terrific kids.

Although Melanie's full time job is Mom, she enjoys writing for children and young adults. She had a story chosen for the book, "Best of the Children's Market" and over thirty stories published in magazines such as *Highlights*, *All About You*, and *Teen*. However, her favorites to write for have always been *The Friend* and *The New Era*.

Melanie enjoys lounging in the bathtub, writing in bed, and living in a home longer than two years.

You can e-mail Melanie at **bymelaniemarks@comcast.net**.